Clara Barnes Martin

Mount Desert on the Coast of Maine

Clara Barnes Martin

Mount Desert on the Coast of Maine

ISBN/EAN: 9783337288518

Printed in Europe, USA, Canada, Australia, Japan

Cover: Foto ©Andreas Hilbeck / pixelio.de

More available books at **www.hansebooks.com**

ON THE

COAST OF MAINE.

"Infinite riches in a little room."

BY

Mrs. CLARA BARNES MARTIN.

SIXTH EDITION.

PORTLAND:
LORING, SHORT & HARMON.
1885.

THE sketch of the topography and history of Mount Desert, which forms the principal part of this little book, includes nearly the whole of a monograph which was written in October, 1866, and first printed, privately, in the following May. The date is of some importance, as parts of it have been so often quoted that they may seem to belong elsewhere than in this their original setting.

To it have now been added some notes upon the routes to Mount Desert and the excursions to be made there, in the hope that it may serve the double purpose of a Guide Book at the Island, and at home in wintry days a souvenir of pleasant summer-time.

MAY, 1885.   C. B. M.

TABLE OF CONTENTS.

ILLUSTRATIONS.

ROUTES TO MOUNT DESERT.

BETWEEN Portland and Mount Desert the traveler has a choice of routes as follows :—

I.

The Maine Central Railroad, *via* Augusta, Waterville, Bangor and Ellsworth to Mount Desert Ferry.

II.

To leave the Maine Central Road at Bath, and take the Knox and Lincoln Road to Rockland ; thence by steamboat.

III.

The ocean route direct from Portland to Rockland, by the Lewiston or the City of Richmond, the large steamboats of the Portland, Bangor, and Machias Steamboat Company.

In this case there is a choice of boats at Portland, one which cares for the permanent business of the year, takes the northern course along the coast by Castine and Sedgwick ; the other, a more southern one, though still within the margin of the islands. There is difference enough between the two to make each worth its turn ;

but the southern course takes less time, as no landing is made between Southwest Harbor and Rockland. Portland is reached in twelve hours from Bar Harbor, and Boston in sixteen.

I.

The Maine Central Railroad passes through the old towns on the shore of Casco Bay, Falmouth, Yarmouth, Freeport, Brunswick, the site of Bowdoin College. The college grounds are east of the station, within two minutes walk. The chapel, library and picture gallery will repay a visit. Thence crossing the Androscoggin, it turns eastward, and strikes the right bank of the Kennebec, giving beautiful views of the river.

Between Pittston and Hallowell the traveler is scarcely out of sight of some of the enormous ice-houses in which a large portion of the annual winter harvest of Maine is stored. Hardly anywhere else in the world is so much of that work done within the same space. Figures are not easy to come at, but the total of the ice-crop of Maine amounts to hundreds of thousands of tons, and its value to millions of dollars.

After passing Hallowell the State Insane Asylum and the United States Arsenal will be seen on the opposite bank of the river. Augusta is the Capital of the State, but the State-house itself is on the high ground to the west, and cannot be seen from the train.

The railroad crosses the river at Augusta, and again at Waterville, in both places just over the falls, giving fine views of the river which as the outlet of Moosehead Lake, is at all seasons of the year a full and rapid stream.

The station at Waterville is directly opposite the grounds of Colby University, a college which has had in its long history an importance within the Baptist denomination, and a place in the annals of the State, much beyond that indicated by the mere numbers of the students. The recent munificent bequest of Governor Coburn has now given it the first rank in the State for wealth.

Beyond Waterville the road crosses directly the rolling but scarcely picturesque country between the Kennebec river and the Penobscot to Bangor. This city numbers about 20,000 inhabitants. It has been for many years a great centre for lumbering operations and is now one of the greatest lumber markets in the world. Its fine well-shaded streets would well repay a drive through them.

Passengers for Mount Desert[1] here leave the trunk road which goes on eastward to Vanceboro and the

---

[1] There is a most delightful alternative upon this route. A steamboat leaves Bangor for Mount Desert every other morning. It touches at the river towns, and then skirts the eastern shore of the Bay. Amid such scenery, a voyage through quiet waters offers the very perfection of traveling.

Provinces. The branch crosses the river to Brewer and runs thence east and south through Ellsworth, Hancock, and Sullivan to Mount Desert Ferry on Frenchman's Bay, seven miles north of Bar Harbor.[2] There are long stretches of country where the bare ledges and thick strewn boulders show that desolation of fire which destroys the very soil itself. Half way between Bangor and Ellsworth the road skirts Phillips' Pond, a favorite resort from Bangor for fishing. It was early stocked with black bass and perch and togue are abundant. Below are Egery's Pond and Stony Pond, and not far from Ellsworth the shire-town of Hancock County, the road crosses the Union River. The necessity of finding a low grade leaves little chance for views along the road. Green Mountain and Newport are visible for a short distance near the Franklin Road and Skillinger's Bay.

A single year has transformed the little rock-edged

---

[2] The stage road from Bangor is not of much interest except for the views of the Mount Desert Hills; one point on ground near Phillips' Pond commands a wide prospect: on the right the Bald Mountain, the Great Mountain in Orland, and Bluehill; on the left are the hills in Aurora, far away the range back of Sullivan, and the Schoodic Mountain; and in front all the bold outline of Mount Desert itself.

The only town of consequence on the route beyond Bangor is Ellsworth, the shire town of Hancock County. Below the town the road passes through a flat country in Trenton to the bridge at Trenton Point, over Mount Desert Narrows. They are not much more than twenty rods wide at high water, and at low tide the passage has sometimes been forded. Not far beyond the bridge the road divides, turning east to Bar Harbor, or keeping south to Somesville.

cove, near Hancock Point, into a busy scene. It is not merely that far the larger portion of the Mount Desert pleasure travel comes this way, but it became at once the point of connection for the Nova Scotia steamboats. The International Line is also to avail itself of the new facilities, so that Mount Desert Ferry is already a port of entry under custom house regulations.

The transit thence to Bar Harbor itself is short and easy, without exposure either to the perils or the disagreeables, of the actual sea. The western mountains on the Island are concealed by the nearer masses of MacFarland's and Great Pond Hill, but Green Mountain and Newport make an impressive background for the village. Blue Hill may be seen in the west directly over the Narrows, the Schoodic Mountain seaward and the Gouldsboro Hills behind Sullivan.

It must be admitted that the old lovers of Mount Desert find this approach a tame affair after the grand and picturesque procession of hills which they have been used to accompany in the voyage round the south of the Island. So much, however, is to be said of the greater certainty and comfort of the railway train that we can only sigh over the past and submit to the inevitable change.

II.

The second route diverges from the Maine Central Road at Bath, and crossing the Kennebec River follows the Knox and Lincoln Railroad to Rockland. The road is built along and across the many inlets that break up the coast of Lincoln County. The old towns of Damariscotta and Wiscasset were busy centres in the great shipbuilding days of Maine. Since those were over, profound quiet had rested upon them until the railroad came to stir a new life. The long, old bridges at Wiscasset, and the woods on the shore beyond, will be recognized as the scene of several chapters of "One Summer."

Thomaston[1] and Rockland are both devoted to the manufacture of lime, and at Rockland are the headquarters of supply for the quarries on the islands in the Bay. One company alone employs 1,800 men.

The steamboat leaves Rockland on the arrival of the train. It takes a southern course across Penobscot Bay to the Fox Island Thoroughfare (landing at North Haven), and crosses Isle au Haut Bay, the eastern ship chanel to the Penobscot. Castine Light-house is on the north. Next comes Deer Island Thoroughfare with two

---

[1] The brick railroad station at Thomaston was once the stable belonging to the mansion of General Knox, of Revolutionary fame.

landings on the west and south of Deer Isle, Burnt Cove and Green's Landing.

Next on the south is Marshall's Island. Then we pass through York Narrows,—Black Island on the north and Swan Island on the south. Thence across Bluehill Bay, the Placentia group of islands lying to the south.

After passing York Narrows the coast of Mount Desert is directly in front with the light-house at Bass Harbor · Head. For the remainder of the route see page 24.

This journey requires less than ten hours from Portland, leaving there by the early morning train. Travelers must leave Boston at the latest by steamboat or train of the previous evening. But on returning, the steamboat leaves Bar Harbor early enough in the morning to enable passengers to reach Boston at 10 P. M. the same evening, thus making the whole trip not more than fifteen hours.

Connection can be made at Rockland with the outside boat direct for Boston; but this should never be attempted without engaging staterooms beforehand, as the boat is always crowded.

III.

By the third route a traveler may leave Boston at 6 P. M. Friday, and arrive at Southwest Harbor at 12 M.

on Saturday, and Bar Harbor at 2 P. M., or if he prefers,
go by Somesville (see page 26). He can have all day
Sunday at Bar Harbor, which, if it be clear, had best be
spent on the mountain,—then can take the boat to return
Monday morning, and reach Boston the same evening.

Those who have enjoyed this trip, on two bright summer days, will agree that nothing could be pleasanter.
Sheltered by outlying islands from the roll of the sea,
the boat passes many a picturesque inlet and sea-side
hamlet. Broad harvest fields alternate with wooded
crag and ledge. The village churches show their spires
afar, and the light-houses shine upon the headlands.
Nor is the scene bereft of story, for—besides Castine,
Isle au Haut and Monts Deserts which keep the memory
of the lost dominion of France—bay and headland, reach
and river, answer to

"Names,
Whose melody yet lingers, like the last
Vibration of the red man's requiem."

It was the opening of this route which made Mount
Desert the popular resort that it is. So long as but one
stage a week connected it with the outside world, only a
few artists or leisurely tourists traveling with their own
horses found their way to its marvels.

The steamboat leaves Portland at 10 P. M., on the arrival of the Boston train. The first landing is at ROCK-

LAND on the Penobscot Bay, which is reached almost before sunrise, except on the shortest summer nights. The sight of the sunrise on the Camden Hills is worth the early rising. •

These hills lie about five miles to the northwest of the steamboat's course in leaving Rockland. They are in reality a series of mountain ranges, highest close to the shore of the Bay, and falling off to the level of the country about five miles inland. The three principal heights, naming them from southwest to northeast, are Ragged Mountain, Bald Mountain, and Megunticook. A smaller hill called Mount Battu lies under Megunticook. It would be seen from the steamboat only in peculiar states of the atmosphere against Megunticook, but from Camden village it is much the more conspicuous. There is a large pond behind the hills and along its shore a fine drive.

Farther up the Bay is Mount Waldo, back of Belfast, and beyond Frankfort the Mosquito Mountain.

This western shore of the Bay presents many of the same combinations of mountain and sea which draw so many people to Mount Desert. That is not a distant future in which this whole coast will become a favorite resort. Not the scenery only, but the climate attracts, a climate in which summer heats are tempered by sea-breezes which have not lost all their bracing vigor, like the enervating atmosphere of more southern coasts.

From ROCKLAND the course lies from eight to fifteen miles farther north than that described on page 16. It is the wonder of this coast that there should be two such inland passages with deep channels and broad reaches, yet so land-locked as to be calm and smooth. It leads through the islands that form the town of Isleborough northward and eastward to CASTINE. It is an unexpected discovery to find the town turning itself from Penobscot Bay and looking out eastward upon a harbor of its

own. A reference to the county map will show how
curiously these inlets separate or penetrate the towns of
Penobscot, Brooksville, and Sedgwick. The drives along
their shores are remarkably picturesque, and no more
agreeable variety for a summer journey could be found,
than to take carriages at Bucksport and follow the shore
of Penobscot Bay to Castine. Then take the road north
again round the Northern Bay and follow the winding
shore of Bagaduce Bay, then across Sedgwick to Bluehill Bay. After such a drive one will no longer wonder
at the statement that there are three thousand miles of
sea-coast between Kittery and Machias.

The old town of CASTINE on the sloping hill-side beside the sheltered harbor seems quiet enough; but no spot in all New England has witnessed more
varying fortune.

Far back in the earliest time (1627) the Plymouth colony had a trading-
house here, but on the restoration of New France and Acadie by Charles to
France, it fell into the hands of D'Aulney de Charnisay, an ambitious and
unscrupulous Frenchman.

East of the St. Croix the land was in possession of Claude La Tour, who,
though a Protestant, seems to have been scarcely less fierce than his neighbor. Between the two a bitter rivalry existed for ten years for a monopoly
of the trade and for the control of the natives. D'Aulney looked for influ-
ence from home in his favor, and enlisted the aid of the Jesuit missionaries,
while La Tour, pleading his Protestantism with the Puritan colonists, more
than once received absolutely vital aid.

There is a woman in the story too,—the wife of La Tour, an accomplished
Frenchwoman, high spirited withal, whose bravery might have saved the
cause of any man less imprudent then her husband.

The quarrel long smouldering blazed into open war in the spring of 1643,
when D'Aulney blockaded La Tour in his own harbor (now St. John, New
Brunswick).

Almost in despair La Tour beheld the arrival of a ship of fugitives from Rochelle outside the enemy's fleet. By night he gained the ship with his wife and sailed for Boston. Once there he induced the colonists to permit him to fit out four ships at his own expense. Away they sailed and attacked D'Aulney to such purpose that he not only raised the blockade, but fled homeward and ran his ships aground (in this very harbor of Castine), the more quickly to defend himself. A sharp skirmish ensued at the mill, in which the Massachusetts men won, and they returned home with a ship taken from D'Aulney laden with a cargo of furs.

A little later a party of Commissioners from Boston were detained by him in defiance of all law or custom, and so exasperated were they, that one of them gathered a small force of discontented spirits and attacked D'Aulney at his farm-house a few miles from the fort. Nothing came of it except the intense wrath of D'Aulney, who vowed he would stop all trade between the colonies and La Tour, and forthwith made prize of every vessel he could lay his hands on. Most of all he hoped to capture La Tour's wife, who was just returning from London, but bitter was his disappointment to learn that after her safe arrival in Boston she had obtained, by much clever management, the means to charter three London ships and to sail for St. John.

Unluckily, it soon came to the ear of D'Aulney that her husband had left her for a cruise in the Bay of Fundy. Off he went, behaving like a pirate on the way: but he had to deal with a woman whose valor was worthy of her Huguenot blood. She returned his fire upon the fort to such good purpose that twenty of his men were killed and his ship barely escaped sinking.

Home he came more angry with Massachusetts than ever. The colony justly accused him of having broken a treaty,—of violating the king's peace; but he retorted with effrontery, and on his own part demanded satisfaction for the aid which had been given Mme. La Tour. Between such implacable rivals it seemed almost impossible to keep the peace with either, but the Governor once more attempted negotiations. Apparently the colonists realized that the nearness to them of the Penobscot trading-house and its violent master, made it more important to treat with him. A considerable sum was awarded him, and then comes one gleam of humor to light up the stormy scene. Over and above the money, so the old chronicles say, the magistrates sent him as a token of their good will "a flattering present,"—"an elegant *sedan*, which being sent by a Mexican Viceroy to his sister in the West Indies," fell into the hands of a captain who had presented it to the Governor. One may well suppose it the first and the last of the kind in the town. Can one fancy the wife and daughter of D'Aulney parading in it from the fort to the farm-house, and from the farm-house to the mill?

But the long delay of the negotiation was fatal to the cause of La Tour. It prevented supplies from reaching him, so that reduced by necessity to set out on a cruise, he left the fort so unprotected that it fell before another attack from D'Aulney. He brought off here, in plunder of all kinds, not less than ten thousand dollars; but his chief prize was the noble wife of La Tour herself. Not long, however, was his triumph. The terror of imprisonment was the last sorrow of her tragic life, and within three weeks she died broken-hearted.

The wretched La Tour sought in vain to atone for his imprudence. He disappeared from the country, leaving, as it seemed, a complete victory to his rival. D'Aulney survived but a few years, apparently having exhausted all his vigor in this bitter personal hatred.

But of all the story, the sequel is the strangest. Not long after the death of D'Aulney, La Tour reappeared and married his widow. Thus he entered into undisturbed possession of both territories. Several children were born to him, and the story ends in the prosperity of a peaceful trading establishment. One last glimpse of the family is given in the will of the daughter of D'Aulney, who became a canoness of St. Omer's and who bequeathed her fortune to her half brothers and sisters, the children of her father's hated rival.

Forty years later the Penobscot trading-house was made the object of mingled jealousy and averice to the English colonists by another Frenchman, him whose name the town now bears.

For something like thirty years the Baron Vincent de Castine lived here, "to the French a mystery, to the colonists a prodigy." A man of education, of noble birth and of courtly manners, he had held a high position in the French army at Quebec, which he suddenly resigned and betook himself to the wilderness. In this lonely spot by the sea, half merchant, half mission-ary, he won from the Indians a loyal devotion such as they gave no other white man. The whole sad tragedy of Indian warfare known as King Wil-liam's War, had its beginning in an outbreak of resentment on their part at an attempt to rob Castine. Again and again, the trading-house was attacked by parties of English on various pretexts, and at one time it was plundered of everything except the plate and ornaments of the little chapel. Never-theless, Castine maintained his position, until about the year 1700 he chose to return to his native Pyrenees, carrying with him a large fortune.

He left behind him a son, "Castine the younger," who, without possessing the strength of character or the fascinating address which had made his father so powerful, proved himself a man of magnanimity and forbearance. His aid was more than once required in difficult negotiations between the French and English, but his departure for France in 1721 severed finally what seems to have been the strongest bond that ever existed between the Indians and the white men in New England.

Sixty years of quiet life pass over the scene, till in 1779 an armed fleet from Halifax enters the harbor. A rude fort is soon built by the soldiers it brings, to the alarm of all the eastern settlements. A hurried and importunate petition is sent to the General Court, and so prompt is the response of Massachusetts that only forty days from the landing of the British a fleet of nineteen armed vessels and twenty-four transports arrives at Bagaduce (as Castine was then called). Peleg Wadsworth the grandfather of the poet Longfellow was second in command. Paul Revere was at the head of the artilery force, and Captain More (afterwards Sir John of Corunna fame) was with the English in the first engagement. One daring attempt is made to storm the fort, which would have been remembered among the most brilliant exploits of the war, had the expedition succeeded.

But never did expedition meet fate more disastrous. Three precious weeks were lost by divided counsels. A fleet from Halifax appeared outside the harbor. In the flight that followed four of the American vessels were captured and the remaining fifteen, including the Warren, a fine new frigate, were either blown up or burnt by their crews at different points along Penobscot Bay, the men escaping, with much suffering, to the towns west and south.

After this fatal disaster the British held undisturbed possession of the peninsula until the close of the war. In fact this garrison was the last to leave the country, not being withdrawn until December, 1783, some weeks after the disbanding of the American Army.

In 1796 the town was laid out and received its present name, but there is still one more story of war connected with it.

In August, 1814, another fleet from Halifax appeared before the town, Frightened by its numbers and strength (there were three seventy-fours and two frigates) the commander blew up the fort, and like the Massachusetts men thirty-five years before, fled up the bay. The British held the place during the remainder of the war, causing the greatest possible annoyance, and even suffering, to the people not only of the town, but of all the country up and down Penobscot Bay.

So ends the curious history which links tranquil, commonplace to-day with the tradition and romance of a far-off time.

From Castine the course lies southward past Cape Rosier through the Eggemoggin Reach, which is like a broad river, varying in width from one to three miles. To the north and east are the towns of Brooksville, Sedgwick, and Brooklin, and on the other side that of Deer Isle, which includes the two islands of that name and a score or more of lesser ones. The two landings are one in Sedgwick and one on the Great Deer Isle.

Emerging from the Reach and passing the light-house on Harbor Island, the Isle au Haut shows far seaward, on the right, the hill[1] which gave it its name. It lies one league directly south of Great Deer Isle and forms the eastern limit of Penobscot Bay, of which White Head, six leagues off, below Rockland, is the western.

Eastward on the left appears the well-wooded slope of the Western Mountain on MOUNT DESERT ISLAND. The steamboat's course lies so directly towards it that it long conceals the rest of the range; but as the boat passes the Placentia group and rounds Bass Harbor Head, one mountain after another comes into view, till just opposite the old church on Cranberry Island, the long line is displayed before the eye, even to the faint edge of farthest Newport.

[1] Height 600 feet.

Nearest at the left is the Western Mountain, then Beech Mountain, both still covered with forest; then Dog Mountain and Robinson's, which make the western wall of Somes' Sound. Next on the east of the Sound is the Brown Mountain. Then rises the vast irregular mass of Sargent, which shows two or three heads. The little Twin nestles by it in the hollow on the southeast. Then comes Pemetic, which keeps in its name the Indian traditions of the Island. Last are the long slopes of Green Mountain, with the Summit House at the top, and the ridge of Newport, just seen against the sky beyond.

The first landing on the island is made at South West Harbor in the town of Tremont. In good weather the steamboat is due here by 12 M. at the latest. The village is the largest as well as the oldest on the Island. Long ago, when Mount Desert was an Ultima Thule, it used to be the resort of small parties of chosen spirits. The traditions of Deacon Clarke's brown bread and clam chowder have become familiar stories; but somewhere there must be journals and note-books out of which might be reproduced against a background of mountain and sea, the portraits of the wise and the fair in the quaint setting of the primitive manners of the time. There are comfortable hotels here now, and not a few prefer the more

2

peaceful life of the genuine seaside village to the gay
crowd at Bar Harbor. [1]

The village of Southwest Harbor, twenty-five years
ago, was close along the east shore, quite away from the
Sound ; but recently several houses have been built upon
commanding points whence the view is a positive revelation as one comes up by the low road from the landing.
From the "Towers" is visible all the range of hills from
west to east, deep cleft by the long stretch of the Sound
which opens to view quite up to the fields at Sargent's
Cove. Farthest to the right, past Bear and Sutton's
islands, stretches the clear-cut line of the open sea. It
is the spot of all others at which it is possible to live
where one can possess at a glance the unique beauty of
the Mount Desert landscape. Here one has it every
hour of daily life ; lives it : needs not to go to see it.

A traveler with but little time to spare (see page 16) might be pleased to
leave the steamboat here.

In good weather the boat arrives in time for dinner, after which, the drive
can be taken round the western shore, about twelve miles (see page 36), or
by the direct road, to Somesville. The choice may then be made,—to take
tea at the Mount Desert House and drive the same evening the seven or eight
miles to Bar Harbor, or to stay and spend the night at Somesville.

After leaving Southwest Harbor the western hills

[1] The etsablishment for canning lobsters has been considered an objection
to the place ; but the increased length of the "close season" and greater care
about the work, have reduced the trouble to almost nothing.

recede, and the remarkable inlet called Somes' Sound opens. The small promontory, the Flying Mountain, juts out across its mouth, but for a short distance there is a view of the steep eastern face of Dog Mountain, and farther inland the Narrows between Robinson's Mountain and Brown. Moving farther eastward, the other Twin comes out from behind Sargent. Dry Mountain separates itself from Green, and Newport's narrow ridge resolves itself into the rounded spurs of its southern face, and so one can count from first to last "the eight or nine notches in the Isle of Mount Desert" which Champlain saw.

Along the shore may be seen some of the spots most frequented by visitors. Close under Green Mountain is the little hamlet of Otter Creek. Just round the point are Otter Cliffs. A mile or so farther, the great cleft known as Thunder Hole, then the bright sands of Newport Beach, and, next that. the frowning bluff of Great Head.

Once past the Head, the beautiful expanse of Frenchman's Bay spreads out before us. Newport Mountain now hides all the others with its steep and rugged cliffs. Now and then there is a glimpse of the Schooner Head road. The Head itself cannot be mistaken on account of the likeness in front of a fore-and-aft schooner with

jib and mainsail set.   Below it at low tide can be seen
the opening into the chasm of the Spouting Horn.   Across
the Cove at low tide also, the dark mouth of Anemone
Cave is visible.

The pretty cottages at Schooner Head warn the traveler that Bar Harbor is near at hand.   There is only
time to look at the other shore of Frenchman's Bay, Iron-
bound Island, and Schoodic Mountain,[1] the blue hills
beyond Sullivan, and to count the five Porcupines.
Opposite Newport Cliffs they lie in a row, with **Bar
Island** at the left and **Bald Porcupine** in the middle.

BAR HARBOR, the little straggling hamlet of twenty
years ago, is now transformed into a crowd of roofs and
towers.   Each new hotel is larger than the last, and every
summer adds something to the possibilities of luxury.
The abundant water of Eagle Lake supplies every need.
The spacious landing, the boats, the bath-houses, the shops,
and, above all, the multitude of horses, are a bewildering
contrast to the quiet and, it must be owned, the incon-
venience of those earlier days.

It is however a mistake to suppose that because Bar
Harbor has become a gay watering-place, Mount Desert
is spoiled for people of more simple and more sober taste.
Bar Harbor and Southwest Harbor added together cover

---

[1] **Height about 400 feet.**

but an insignificant portion of the whole island. The gain in convenience and comfort is felt everywhere, and only a little care in choosing will secure the retirement and the rest which very many people prefer in a summer holiday.

TOPOGRAPHY AND HISTORY.

An island, full of hills and dells,
    All rumpled and uneven
With green recesses, sudden swells,
    And odorous valleys driven
So deep and straight, that always there
The wind is cradled to soft air.

E. B. Browning.

THE traveler along the Atlantic coast, whether by land or sea, cannot have failed to notice its monotonous character. With scarcely an exception, long beach and flat marsh extend from the coral reefs of Florida to the granite headlands of Cape Ann. Then again the sand reappears as far as Portland, when the whole aspect changes. Bold bluff and rugged cliff make the fiords of Maine the wonder and delight of artist and tourist. For a thousand miles, round

> "winding shores
> Of narrow capes and isles, which lie
> Slumbering to Ocean's lullaby"—

stretches the stern and rock-bound coast. At first there is in the Casco and Kennebec Bays, a picturesque charm, which allies the shore with the rich farms lying inland, but as we approach the Penobscot, grander outlines press upon the view. Hill and mountain crowd down to the sea, and eastward rises

> "The gray and thunder-smitten pile
> Which marks afar the Desert Isle."

The exact expression of the special character of Mount Desert, which as it were, culminates the wonder of the coast, involves antitheses and contrasts oftener employed in the creations of poetic fancy, but here, absolutely necessary to convey any adequate idea of the country. Bleak mountain-side and sunny nook in sheltered cove; frowning precipice and gentle, smiling meadow; broad, heaving ocean and placid mountain lake; dashing sea-foam and glistening trout brook; the deep thunder of the ground-swell, and the solemn stillness of the mountain gorge: the impetuous rush and splash of the surf and the musical cadence of far-off water-falls. all mingle and blend in the memory of this wonderful land.

It is difficult to make such a peculiar topography understood even with the aid of a map, but some conception of it may be formed from the following facts :—

The Island lies one hundred and ten miles east of Portland and so near the main-land as to be separated from it, on the north, only by a narrow arm of the sea which is crossed by the Trenton bridge. It covers a hundred square miles and includes three towns. The southern is named Tremont; the second, in which are most of the mountains, Mount Desert, and the third and northern, chiefly on the low land, is the last that one would expect to find on *Mount Desert* Island, "Eden" itself.

Its greatest length is fourteen miles in a line running a little east of north, from Bass Harbor Head to Salisbury's

Cove, and its greatest breadth eight miles on a line directly west from Schooner Head on Frenchman's Bay. Its harbors have been long well known. Two of them on the south shore are named, somewhat to the perplexity of travelers, respectively Southwest and Northeast. The fact that the names are given in reference to their positions on either side of the entrance to Somes' Sound explains the anomaly. A third, Bar Harbor, is on Frenchman's Bay on the northeast side of the island, and is formed, as its name implies, by the bar which unites one of the Porcupine Islands with Mount Desert. The village at this harbor is the place of greatest resort. It lies scattered along the shore, and, with the harbor and islands, makes a most charming picture as seen from the mountains behind it.

The mountains are upon the southern half of the Island and lie in seven ridges, running nearly north and south. Geologically speaking,[1] they form one end of an immense horseshoe of granite, which re-appears on the mainland in Sullivan, runs north about thirty-five miles, returns southward through Bluehill and terminates on Deer Isle,

---

[1] The curious in such things will be interested to find the traces of glacial action which are left in many parts of the Island. The rocks at the Spouting Horn show the scratches very plainly, and on Green Mountain, "all the way up the last slope, wherever the rock is exposed, may be seen well-engraved, flat surfaces of rose-colored protogyne, on which the scratches and grooves sometimes run for twenty feet without any perceptible interruption."— AGASSIZ.

about twenty-five miles from Mount Desert. The great basin within is filled with the later and lighter formations known as schists. The granite and sienite which are rather indeterminately distributed are in some places of the finest quality, but unfortunately, on this Island, too hard for quarrying. The pink feldspar is often so abundant as to give the rocks a warm tint. The western sides of the mountains slope gradually upward to the summit but on the east, all of them descend by steep, sheer precipices,—and more remarkable still,—four of them into deep lakes, and a fifth into Somes' Sound, which is an arm of the sea seven miles long, and at the Narrows a hundred and forty feet deep.

The general formation of the mountain ridges is curiously repeated in the low hills round Bar Harbor, and again in the northwest near High Head. The Porcupine Islands are the same thing, being only tops of similar steep-faced hills.

A cross-section, eastward, through the mountains from just above Seal Cove, will perhaps make most plain "the lay of the land." The lowland margin is here a mile and a quarter wide. Then comes Seal Cove Pond, two miles long, noted for white perch of goodly size and flavor. Then a mountain range ; next, Long Pond, five miles long, and reminding one of the Penobscot River Narrows.

Next to this lie Beech Hill and Beech Hill Ridge. (See page 93.)

From this ridge is a fine western view, and it is very easy of access, being not more than two miles from Somesville. Deming's Pond lies in the shadow of Beech Hill Cliffs, and the road from Somesville to Southwest Harbor runs along its eastern shore. The third ridge consists of two very distinct mountains, the lower one being Dog Mountain, already mentioned as bordering on the Sound. Its eastern face is probably the most remarkable point on the Island, being an almost perpendicular descent of six hundred feet, and this too, be it remembered, into the waters of the Sound, at its very foot. To some persons, this Sound is the greatest wonder of all, and there is an irresistible fascination about sailing upon it. Its narrow length and lofty shores make it subject to dangerous squalls, but, with a skillful hand to veer the sail, nothing could be more delightful than the morning we spent upon its waters, floating—no whence, no whither— now drifting on a sea of glass, now scudding swiftly before brisk breezes—guiding our little boat under the birchen shadows of the Narrows, or pausing, awe-struck, under the dark frown of the cliff, while the great bald eagle sailed over our heads and the solemn echoes rolled grandly above the murmur of the pines. East of the Sound another mountain rises. Then comes a valley, in which

the road leaves, on either side, a bright pond. Next is
Sargent, a mountain of a breadth and massive proportion
which materially lessens the effect of its height, so that
it is only after some study and comparison from different points that its really grand outlines are appreciated.
Southeast of Sargent is the mountain which bears the
old Indian name, Pemetic. It is the third in the great
trio, being upwards of twelve hundred feet high. It is
most effectively seen from the road between Bar Harbor
and Somesville, and is remembered for its sharp, serrated
edge against the sky. Close beneath it on the east is the
little Turtle Lake, more than three hundred feet above
the level of the sea. Its outlet is through Eagle Lake
on the north, and so out by Duck Brook. To the west,
Pemetic overshadows Jordan's Pond, at the head of which
are the two hills known as the Twins, or, on the map, the
Bubbles. The approach to it is on the south from the
sea. With the Twins beyond and the loftier ranges on
either side, the lake sparkles in its rugged mountain setting—the Diamond of the Forest. The Twins themselves are of an exquisite grace and suggest the tender-
est simile. Vainly I tried to sketch the sunset shadows
upon them and the long light across the lake, till the twilight gathered and the lone call of the loon sounded in
the air.

The outlet of the pond is through another small one

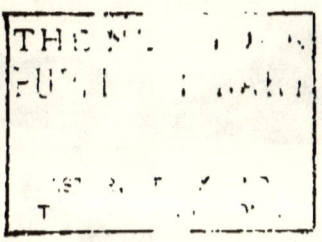

near the shore, so that there is a chain of four, except that it is broken by the northern slope of Pemetic, so that two flow south and two north. The most northern is Eagle, much resorted.to from Bar Harbor for boating. It lies high, but seems at the outlet to be in a comparatively low country and then to run up under the hills. They group about it in such mass and sweep as to give an effect much beyond their real size. Seen from the water under a drifting thunder-cloud, they come out in a startling silhouette of black on gray that makes a very grand picture.

Eastward still is Green Mountain or "Adam's Grave,"[1] —the longest and largest, as well as highest mountain on the island. It extends six miles from Duck Brook to Otter creek, and has a bold spur on the northeast, which is sometimes separately distinguished as the Dry Mountain.

The reader who has followed me thus far, must already have divined something of the unparalleled wonder of the view from the summit. Half ocean, half land, and the middle distance a bright mosaic of island and bay,— it stretches northward to far Katahdin, a hundred and twenty miles as the crow flies. Whittier, who, of all our poets, best expresses the spirit of New England scenery,

[1] Thirty years ago, some gentlemen of the Coast Survey, finding the mountains lay just *outside* of Eden, named them "Adam's Grave," Eve's, etc.

thus describes it in his legend of "Mogg Megone" :—

"Beneath the westward turning eye
A thousand wooded islands lie,—
Their thousand tints of beauty glow
Down in the restless waves below.

"There sleeps Placentia's group—
There, gloomily against the sky
The Dark Isles rear their summits high;
And Desert Rock, abrupt and bare,
Lifts its gray turrets in the air,—
Seen from afar, like some stronghold
Built by the ocean kings of old;
And, faint as smoke wreath, white and thin,
Swells in the north vast Katahdin;
And, wandering from its marshy feet,
The broad Penobscot comes to meet
And mingle with his own bright bay."

Two days unite in my recollection of the scene ; one, the clearest and brightest of all that year, when Katahdin's broad pyramid rose on the utmost horizon, "the distinctest mountain on all this side the continent," and, opposite, not a ripple stirred the halcyon sea,—far,—far off,—till the eye failed for seeing. Three years later, low soft clouds narrowed the view, and we climbed round the mountain's brow looking down into the gorges below, and watched the showers passing by, till the sun came out beyond them, and though all the land was gray through the intervening rain—bay and river shone like molten silver that glowed to gold as the sunset glory came on, and the King of day shot forth a lurid crimson glare, then suddenly vanished into night. Then, turning seaward, we counted each

> "Lonely coast-light set
> Within its wave-washed minaret."

Five of them glimmered or flashed along the shore, and the farthest of all as it hung in mid-air, the beacon on Mount Desert Rock, twinkled like a star. As the evening air grew chill we gathered round the cheery claze of the cottage fire, and a late-comer from the world below told us the tale of Heart's Content.[1]

The brief summer night waned speedily, and at four o'clock we were summoned to see the sun rise. Alas! that mountain sunrises should be so uncertain! My friend had spent the night alone in the old Coast Survey Observatory five years before, and daylight found him surrounded by a dense fog. This time we fared little better, for all the much-desired splendor ended in—

> "Red sky in the morning,
> Sailors take warning"—

and the rain began to fall. Fearing to be detained by a veritable storm, two of us left the cottage at ten minutes past five, and walking all the way reached our house in Bar Harbor at seven. The shower ceased shortly after we started, and among the pleasantest of my memories is that fresh morning walk, as we passed

[1] The successful landing of the Atlantic Cable of 1866.

under the soft grey light in the stillness of the woods, brushing the gossamer from before our faces, while the squirrels chirped over our heads or skipped,—one,—two,—three,—across our path, and the early songs of the birds rang above us. One of them, of three sweet, slow notes, then the same repeated rapidly, ended with a gladsome twitter that went to one's very heart.

Another visit in 1883 proved that the whole of a mid-summer day is not long enough to grow weary in, while watching the landscape under the drifting sunshine and shadows. Eight " coast lights" now are visible from the Summit House, and through the great windows of the parlors, one can follow the sweep of the stars, while the fire glows upon the wide hearth. The night was abso-lutely quiet and at day-light the next morning we were again wrapped in dark gray fog. Yet, by five o'clock the July sun was broad and hot in the east, but never had mist undergone a more wonderful transformation. Below us all around lay an immense plain of white, dazzling untrodden snow. Near us not a leaf was stir-ring. The air was warm and still, while up out from beneath the snow came the morning song of the birds.

Between Green Mountain and Newport is the valley well known as the Gorge. The road from Bar Harbor to Otter Creek runs through it. The stranger to Mount Desert, remembering the Flume or the Crawford Notch, would disallow its claim to grandeur if I gave for it only heights and distances. It is not in itself alone that the Gorge is so remarkable, but that such a valley should lie so near the ocean. The cliffs that wall it in overlook the opean sea. The bubbles in the brook that sparkles by us will in an hour be lost in the surf, and the splash and ripple of the cascade afar upon the mountain side chords with the deep monotone of the ground swell. The narrowest part of the Gorge is three miles from Bar Harbor. The drive is pleasantest in the afternoon, when the western shadows are long.

Last of all is the Newport Mountain, on which is a small pond. The eastern side of this mountain borders the Schooner Head Road. Like all the eastern faces of the mountains, its cliffs are steep and rugged. The rise in "grim rampart and solid bastion" against the fury of the eastern gales.

This completes the cross-section of the Island, and brings us to the eastern shore.

The Coves and Headlands at this side of the Island are of special interest. The view up Frenchman's Bay from any point is fine, and where it includes the five small islands called the Porcupines, is of singular beauty. At Schooner Head, four miles from Bar Harbor, are the Spouting Horn and the Anemone Cave, each alone worth a long journey to see. The Head derives its name from the likeness on its front of a fore-and-aft schooner with jib and mainsail set. The Spouting Horn is a cleft in the rock at the summit of the Head. At its bottom, a passage, worn through a softer rock, opens out to low water mark. The surf boils and seethes through this opening, and at certain times of the tide, when the southeast wind prevails, it rushes up through the Horn with deafening roar, and with terrific force is dashed many feet above the tops of the trees.

Southward, across the Cove, is the Oven,[1]—a huge cave, hollowed out by the waves, and accessible only at low tide. Passing over the rocks above it late one afternoon, when the black waves nearly filled its yawning mouth, it seemed the abode of all grim deaths and desolations; but when the morning sun shone into it and we climbed down across the dripping weeds,—lo! a fair garden at our feet. O marvel of radiant life beneath the sea! Each tiny cleft was alive. In one alone which I could cover with my hand, were seven anemones, while the broad rock pool on the floor of the cavern, enameled with pink and pale green, was crowded with every beautiful variety of them, from wee, white daisy buds to the great tawny creature whose broad side, striped with amber and crimson, covered my palm. In among them

[1] The Devil's Oven was the old popular name, a token of that same sense of the supernatural which found expression in the Diableretz or the Drachenfels of the old world.

nestled all the strange creations of this wondrous sea life,—as safe in their stormy home as the violet beneath the pine. The sunlight reflected from the blue waves shone on the dark vault above us, as through broad glowing window down cathedral nave, and sitting there, one Sunday morning, with wind and wave and echo for organ roll, we sang the "Old Hundredth."[1]

A mile and a half from Schooner Head is Great Head. It is the point of the Island farthest to the southeast and most exposed to the open ocean. It has often been sketched and painted, but no description can do justice to its savage grandeur. It is not to its height alone that it owes its impressiveness, but to the peculiarly massive formation of the rocks,—the overhanging of the whole cliff, and the neverceasing beat and roar of the waves below. Though there is very deep water at its base, it would be almost impossible to land there, even in calm weather.[2]

---

[1] Such was Anemone Cave twenty-two years ago. The eagerness of early visitors stripped it of the wonderful life it sheltered in 1863, but of late, the care of the owner has taught a better sense of the respect due such a treasure—house, and the young anemones are now growing again. But alas! it will take scores of years to restore its beauty.

[2] "Full on the coast the great waves' thunder-shocks
Roll, and afar the wet foam-vapors fall.
No roadstead there, no haven seemed at all,
Nor shelter where a ship might rest at ease;
But from the main earth darted a wild wall of headlands."
A whole volume of poetry might be gathered to illustrate Mount Desert

The tourist should take the shore between the two Heads, either in going or coming, for every step is interesting. He will especially notice, besides Anemone Cave, the curious conglomerate bowlders scattered along; the white birches above a grassy bank in the cove; a rift in the rocks where the waves dash under with a sound like a distant salvo of artillery; and a castellated crag, overgrown with a gray lichen, which perfectly resembles a hoary ruin, clad with ivy,—gray, not green.

A little to the west of Great Head, and in the strongest possible contrast to it, is Sandy or Newport Beach, which borders a pretty natural meadow. From this point, the western view of the lower spurs of Newport Mountain is very beautiful, when the afternoon shadows bring out the cliffs and ravines. To reach the Head by the road the wagons are left at the house above the beach. The path turns to the left going almost to the east shore, then turns to the right. In early summer before it is well-worn it would not be amiss to take a guide. The Head can be reached from the beach by climbing along the rocks, but it is a difficult thing to do.

scenery, but the Guide Book must only permit itself this bit, to bring to mind how the old is still the ever-new, and how fresh and true the words of that morning of the world still are for our far-off western shore. 1877.

The forest primeval is all gone; but huge stumps and scathed trunks show what the axe and the fires have done. The three western mountains and the Twins are covered with a second growth, but the other summits are bleak and bare. The forest-covered hollow at the south end of the Western Mountain was the site of a large steam-mill burned nearly twenty years since. The story of its fate, remote, alone, on a winter's night, makes from the lips of the islanders, a tale only less graphic than that now passing from the memory of the living, of the terrible fire which swept the Island a generation ago. In the valleys and on the open land there is a larger proportion of the more graceful forest trees than is common upon the coast. The Norway pine, the larch, the hemlock, the white cedar, (the arbor vitæ of the garden), and the white birch are all abundant. Could a gentleman transfer to his park the woods of Bar Island, they would be the envy of all his neighbors. One, wise in the secrets of Flora, spoke of disappointment in finding so few of her rarer treasures: but, to me, who am only a lover of flowers, my old favorites of field and wood were never so fair. In early summer the twin-flower carpets the roadside with its tiny leaves and bells, and the low wet meadow south of Salisbury's Cove is covered with the deep maroon of the pitcher plant, and gay with the brilliant purple arethusa and its kindred. Never since

my childhood have I seen such stalwart brakes, fairly
roofing in the forest dells. Then, such white arrow-
heads in the brook—and such roses, crimson and gold,
grow by the way. How often on the shore we gathered
the fragile bells of the blue campanula, and bound them
with long sprays of pink morning-glories, as fair and as
delicate as they! In the ponds are water lilies, yellow
and white, and one, west of Somesville, is all starred
over, as the fields with the dandelions in the spring!
Walking near by on a lonely forest-road, one day, we
came suddenly upon a little sun-lit pool, scarce larger
than a lady's shawl might cover, in the centre of which,
surrounded by attendant buds, shone the broad white
chalice of a single pond-lily. Supreme in her pure
beauty, this queen of the New England Flora held her
sylvan court, while the tall flags in brown furred helmets
kept stately watch and ward around her. The blackberry spreads its snowy flowers in such profusion over
bush and stone wall as for the moment quite to equal in
beauty the clematis of southern New England. The
raspberry grows thickly in the newly cleared fields and
everywhere on moss and under brake glows the red
bunchberry. The whortleberry and the mountain cranberry figure in the earliest traditions of the Island, and
time seems to have wrought no change in their number
or their flavor.

I had hoped for a few paragraphs from my friends "Piscator" and "Venator" concerning their respective pursuits; but failing these, I must record a few hints from memory. There are deer, as might be supposed, in these large forests, protected as they have been from the ravages of the wolves by their separation from the main-land. It is, perhaps, fortunate for them that the best season to hunt them is after the summer travel is over. Their numbers have heretofore been considerably diminished by reckless attacks upon them in the winter when the snow renders them helpless. It is gratifying now to observe, under effective game-laws, the growth of a wholesome public opinion against such slaughter. In the northwest of the Island about Indian Point and High Head are the haunts of the fox. The dogs which are often met when driving in that neighborhood, are kept for hunting them.

The bald eagles are frequently seen, soaring high in the air, or perched on some lofty crag, suggesting tragic stories of child-stealing, or the like—but, luckily for the sheep-folds, no nobler deeds of prowess are on record concerning them, than their habitual robery of the fish-hawks and an occasional raid upon the hen-roosts. At Somesville, we often saw at sunset the tall cranes, sentinel-like on the water's edge, curving their long necks as

3

they watched for their prey, or stretching their awkward legs and spreading their wings for the homeward flight.

Of the trout, we have already spoken. The keenest lovers of the gentle craft prefer the brooks, as affording the finest sport, though the largest fish are found in deep holes in the ponds, to which a guide is necessary. Worms or fresh-water smelts are used for bait in that case, and there is at least a suggestion of too close a likeness to the common trade of cod-fishing. Even in the brooks, I am told, the fish are not susceptible to the elegances of fly-fishing, but rise, at any rate in August, more readily to the vulgar attractions of worms or grasshoppers. It will not take long to exhaust the present supply of fresh water fish, but it will soon be worth while to stock the lakes and brooks. If it is skillfully done, a great variety of sport might be provided, and it will once more be true that trout and cod are caught at Mount Desert by the same hand in one morning.

Of the ocean *per se*, little has been said. Perhaps there is no need, since it is ever the same in all its infinite variety and capability. As all along the shore north of Cape Cod, it is too cold for much enjoyment in sea bathing, but indefatigable ladies do take their daily baths at Bar Harbor. It is hardly necessary to add that there is every opportunity for sea-fishing. Those curious in such things may even assist in taking up the lobster pots, or the emptying of the weirs. A ledge a mile south of Schooner Head is mentioned as an unusually good fishing-ground. One of the most noted excursions is from Bar Harbor, across Frenchman's Bay to Gouldsborough, where there is a drive along the coast which commands fine views of the Mount Desert Hills. In the old times many an anxious night was spent by friends, waiting for the becalmed, or the wind-delayed yachts to return, for it was rare to have a favoring breeze both to go and to return, but now the steam launches make the excursion easily and surely and almost too rapidly.

The "circular" excursions are by no means confined to the land. Steamboats make daily trips around Frenchman's Bay, going over to South Gouldsboro', then crossing westward to Lamoine above the Ovens, next by Hancock Point to Sullivan. Thence they return to Bar Harbor calling only on the Northwest shore, but making in all a circuit of thirty-five miles at least. There are little steamboats which can be chartered for the excursion entirely round the Island. All other things aside, it is worth the doing, to watch the mountains as they change in outline and creep by each other. The morning boats for Portland give the opportunity to go round to Southwest Harbor and to return by the Bangor boat at night, or, the boats connecting with Mount Desert Ferry make the trip and return in much less time.

This sail between Bar and Southwest Harbors gives, on the whole, the most perfect single idea of the outlines and expanse of the mountain ranges. To accomplish it safely, requires not only experience in sailing, but a special knowledge of the coast, for there are several dangerous sunken ledges in the way. Two or three of them are covered, even at low tide, making no show for even half an hour at a time ; and then a great wave will come over them, which would easily upset a large boat. The shadows on the hills add so much to the beauty of the landscape, that one should choose, if possible, the very early morning or the later half of the afternoon.

The trip to Mount Desert Rock, from Southwest Harbor, is too long and too rough for many to enjoy it, but the very exposure offers an attraction. The rock is but a low ledge in open ocean less than half an acre in extent, about twenty miles south of the Harbor. It has upon it only the light house which was built in 1830. The tower is sixty feet high. The light, a first class one, is seventy feet above the sea level. The Rock can be seen from the top of Green Mountain as a faint grey line, some little distance below the horizon. From the old Summit House it lay directly over the light house on Baker's Island. It is impossible to land upon it except in calm weather, and no one would venture to tarry for fear of a storm. The light-keeper and his assistants are furnished with provisions to last from November to May, and rarely have any communication with the mainland meanwhile.

THE SEA-WALL is two miles south of Southwest Harbor. No figures in feet or rods make any picture of it; but it may suffice to say that the wall extends across several coves for more than a mile. It is fifteen feet high, and in some places ten rods wide. It is composed of bowlders of different sizes, washed up by the sea in some time out of mind. Beautiful specimens of green feldspar, a somewhat rare mineral, are found in the ledges underlying the wall. There is another bit of similar wall east of Northeast Harbor, on the top of which runs the highway.

This catalogue of points of interest might, even now, be more extended, and every year will add to the number; but enough has been said to justify the admiration of returning tourists, and to give some certain information to those to whom Mount Desert is only a name.

The Island first appears in history included in the vast tracts of land, which rival sovereigns of Europe portioned out with studied disregard of each other's claims. One old chronicle quaintly tells how Sir Humphrey Gilbert, at Newfoundland, "issued a general summons to the thirty-six vessels there assembled, and pronounced the authority of good Queen Elizabeth. Her claim to dominion over the sea and over the wilderness, over the whales and over the savages, was promulgated in a solemn and awful manner, and they then departed, each one to his own concerns." Almost in the same year Henry Fourth of France granted to the Sieur De Monts, Acadie, "from the fortieth to the forty-sixth degree of north latitude," or from Philadelphia to Quebec.

From the voyages of this De Monts and of his associates and successors, Mount Desert derives all the human interest of those early years. Champlain first named it "Monts Deserts," from its wild and savage solitudes; and the name Frenchman's Bay, now applied only to the water lying immediately north and east of this island, then belonged to the whole expanse eastward to the Bay of Fundy. The name perpetuates the memory of the sore strait to which came one Nicolas D'Aubri, a priest, who accompanied De Monts in his first voyage. Being one of a party who left their boat to explore the forest, he dropped his sword by a brook where they stopped to drink. Returning to find it he soon lost his way; and his companions, after vain efforts to rescue him, were obliged to leave him to his fate. For sixteen days the poor priest wandered along the shore nearly starved, till he was discovered by a party who had returned to the spot in search of reputed gold and silver, and was carried back to his companions, who received him as one from the dead. This story, it may be added is given upon the authority of one of the early historians of Maine. Remembering what war of words has arisen concerning the planting of settlements but little farther west, these traditions are proffered, subject to such amends as more able research may supply.

Mount Desert itself was the scene of events which, though but an episode in the history of New France, were significant, as embodying all the elements which engendered and embittered the strife of a hundred years between the French and English on the Western Continent. Colonies had been planted prior to 1610 on the St. Croix and at Port Royal. Their appeals to the French Court for aid drew the attention of the Jesuits to this new field. More zealous, we may be sure, for the aggrandizement of their order than for the salvation of the savages, they insisted that two at least of their society should accompany the owner of Port Royal in spite of his ill-concealed dissatisfaction, on his return to the colony. Dissensions early arose. Poutrincourt plainly told them "it was his part to *rule them* on the earth, and theirs, to guide him to heaven." Fortune frowned upon priest and people alike, and the little handful of colonists were reduced almost to utter misery when a ship arrived from France bringing another priest,

Gilbert du Thet, and materials to found a special missionary station.

The Jesuits at home had not been idle and had enlisted in their behalf the enthusiasm of Madame de Guercheville, a lady famed among the attendants of Marie de Medicis, alike for her beauty and her chastity. To her, De Monts transferred his grant, and Louis Thirteenth added to it all North America, from the St. Lawrence to Florida. By subscription from her companions at court, "glad rather to win heaven for the heathen than to merit it for themselves," this ship had been fitted out to plant the cross in the wilds of Acadie. Biard and Masse having joined them at Port Royal, they pursued their voyage toward the Penobscot, but heavy weather drove them close upon the land, the fog came round and after a night of terror lest they should be dashed upon the rocks, they found themselves, when morning dawned, under the cliffs of Mount Desert. It is agreed they must first have landed on the eastern end of the island, somewhat south of Bar Harbor. No attempt, so far as I know, has been made to locate the precise spot, but the cove at Schooner Head seems as likely as any to have been the scene of their landing. Protected a little by reefs from the storm, yet not so difficult of access that they might not have drifted into it, it must have been the most inviting spot on all that coast. Though the sheer precipices of Newport Mountain rise close at hand, and the old forest then, no doubt, shadowed the cove, yet a little pond a few rods from the shore feeds a brook large enough in the spring, even now, to turn a mill. And it is probable that the fields, which are now among the smoothest and best on the island, replace the natural pasture on which the Jesuits raised their cross, when they named the place Saint Sauveur in gratitude for their escape from the storm. They soon heard from the Indians of a more desirable site beside a quiet sea, whereon to build their houses. Biard describes it as three leagues from their first landing-place and on the shore of "The Pool."

Here, accounts differ concerning the length of their stay, but all agree as to the cruel end. According to one tradition they remained five years and built "fortified habitations." Madame de Guercheville had furnished them with both ammunition and stores and farming implements, as well as with means sufficient for performing the offices of the Church. The Indians across the Sound might hear

"The chant of many a holy hymn,
The solemn bell of vespers ringing."

"A rude and unshapely chapel stands,
Built up in that wild by unskilled hands;
Yet the traveler knows it a place of prayer,
For the holy sign of the cross is there;

And should he chance at that place to be,
Of a Sabbath morn, or some hallowed day,
When prayers are made, and masses are said,
Some for the living and some for the dead,
Well might the traveler start to see
The tall, dark forms, that take their way
From the birch canoe, on the river-shore,
And the forest paths to that chapel door;
And marvel to mark the naked knees
And the dusky forheads bending there,
While, in coarse white vesture, over these,
In blessing or in prayer,
Stretching abroad his thin, pale hands,
Like a shrouded ghost, the Jesuit stands."

Whether their destruction came sooner or later, it was complete. Argall, afterwards lieutenant governor of South Virginia, had fitted out an armed vessel, to fish on the New England Coast. He was driven in the fog as far north as Maine. There he heard of Saint Sauveur from the Indians. Strong in the cause of King and Protestant, and yet stronger in the might of his fourteen guns, he sailed down upon the ill-fated colony, and by a single broadside made himself its master. Du Thet was killed; the friendly Indians scattered; their stores rifled and destroyed; Masse, with a few companions, left in the woods to the almost desperate chance of finding their way back to Port Royal, and Biard and the remainder, like the villagers of Grand-Pré, carried off to the English colonies.

So passed away St. Sauveur. The chance and change

of two hundred and fifty years could leave little trace of its site. The local tradition attaches itself to Fernald's Point on the western side of Somes' Sound, about two miles from Southwest Harbor. Biard's narrative gives a few hints from which a theory as to its position may be derived. He writes of a black, rich, fertile soil, a little hill which sheltered them from the northeast wind, and abundant living water at hand. We drove down to the point one morning to verify the description for ourselves. The little hill is, in fact, the Flying Mountain, a bold promontory joined to the eastern spur of Dog Mountain by a narrow isthmus, on which are Mr. Fernald's pastures. His farm lies principally south of the hill, and is considered one of the best on the island; to which result "the black, rich, and fertile soil" no doubt contributes, but more likely his success is due, in the main, to his appreciation of the value of sea-manures. There is a spring at high water mark on each side of the Point, and a brook runs from the mountain through the pasture. The mountains in Biard's day were covered with a heavy hard-wood growth, and as the sound is here completely landlocked, the Point and Cove would offer the most tempting shelter to the storm-tost missionaries.

About half way across the isthmus and a little up the hill, so as to command the water on either side without losing its shelter, are two holes in the ground which are shown as the ruins of the Frenchmen's cellars. They are a few rods apart, running north and south, ten to twelve feet long at present, from two to three feet deep, and of varying width. They seem to have been gradually filled in from the hill above. They are grass-grown, and the very day of our visit in 1866 a spruce, some eight inches in diameter, had been cut down in one of them. The old man who was our guide said the cellars were there in the time of his grandfather who was the first settler, and *he* always said that they were the remains of the French Colony. Our guide seemed anxious to prove that it was not strange that they had filled up so much in two hundred and fifty years, but it is surely stranger still that *any trace* of them is left. My companion was stoutly incredulous, averring that they were only "holes in the ground," and that a little digging would prove that there is no stone work whatever about them. It is a little singular that no antiquarian has attempted to dig them out and restore them. It is certain they are very conveniently situated for such speculations. Stories of the discovery of gold buried by the French are rife, like those of pirates' treasure farther south. A bank of shells near Northeast Harbor probably marks the neighborhood of an Indian village ; and Indian relics of various sorts are not uncommon.

To return to the history; new interests had arisen at home, and the high-handed outrage seems to have been but feebly resented on the one hand, and scarcely justified on the other. No attempt was made to renew the settlement till one Cadilliac received from Louis Fourteenth a grant containing one hundred thousand acres, bordering for two leagues on the bay near Jordan's River on the main-land, and the same on Mt. Desert Island, including the smaller islands lying in the bay. Cadilliac made a resolute effort to hold his ground, but abandoned it in 1713, after the session of the whole territory of Acadie to England, by the treaty of Utrecht. Though afterwards in stations of importance, and at one time governor of Louisiana, he retained with proud affection the memory of his island dominion, and to the day of his death wrote himself "Lord of Mount Desert."

Once more the French appear upon the scene, in the persons of Monsieur and Madame de Gregoire, the latter a granddaughter of Cadilliac. In 1785, they laid their claim to the lands of her ancestor before the General Court of Massachusetts. The property had been included in the estate of Governor Bernard, and though confiscated during the Revolution, had been restored to his son. Nevertheless, such was then the amicable feeling toward France in New England, that the General Court, "to cultivate mutual confidence and union between the subjects of His Most Christian Majesty and the citizens of this State," listened to the appeal, naturalized Monsieur and Madame Gregoire and quit-claimed to them all but lots of a hundred acres each for actual settlers. It is doubtful if they possessed the elements of character essential to success on such a soil in such a climate, for within ten years they sold most of the land to William Bingham of Philadelphia ;[1] but they continued to live for the remainder of their lives at Hull's Cove, which they had made their home. They died about 1810. and stories of their life and manners are repeated to tourists, though the descendant of the nobles of the *ancien régime* would scarce know herself in the "Madam Griguire" of the fishermen's tale. Their graves are shown just outside the little cemetery at the Cove,—outside, because. as the tradition runs. Protestant zeal would not admit the Catholics within. But to them, all spots unblessed by priest with book and prayer

[1] This gentleman had previously acquired considerable possessions in this part of the Province of Maine. One of the earliest grants in what is now Hancock County was of six townships on the condition of their being settled within a specified time by Protestants, a curious little reminder that the earliest settlers had been good Roman Catholics. In 1786, the General Court put into a lottery fifty townships between Penobscot Bay and Passamaquoddy. 165,280 acres were drawn at an average price of fifty-two cents per acre. The greater portion of what was left was bought by Bingham. Of the land purchased from the Gregoires, a piece bordering the Schooner Head road was in 1883 still in possession of his heirs.

and cross were alike, and they sleep quietly, the last relics of French dominion on these shores.[1]

Since the days of the Gregoires, the history of the island seems to have lost its romantic element, and lapses into the ordinary life of a lumbering and fishing community.[2] There seems, on the whole, a steady growth in population and prosperity, though the old men talk of the golden days of their youth, when the forests were yet thick and tall. Large ships were then built, not in one, but in many of the coves of the island, and many a gallant bark sailed to foreign seas, owned and manned at Mount Desert. A few forsaken houses, and here and there one left to grow old half finished, are the only visible signs of a change of fortune, and these are more than made good by new elsewhere. The varied purposes for which the second growth may be used, keep the mills

[1] A more credible account of the position of the graves is, that though the present fence includes them, for many years there was no inclosure whatever there, and when it was first made the fence was built inside them by mistake. A white wooden cross has lately been placed at their heads. 1874.

[2] In the old records of a Massachusetts family has been found the following entry:—

"1808, August 22d. Stephen Badlam, 4th, sailed for Mt. Desert to quiet the settlers on their lots under authority of government with Col. Charles Turner, Jr., and Salem Towne, Jr. Took a plan of the place." The identical plan is still extant. It embraces all the western part of the Island north to a line drawn from what is now called Clark's Cove to Somes' Harbor on the Sound. The "lots" are given with the names of the settlers. They lie along the southwest shore of Southwest Harbor, and along the east shore of Bass Harbor and down towards the Head. 1880.

busy when the ponds and brooks are high, but fishing is the main business of life,—for cod or herring at the east, or for the menhaden at home. The more intelligent and enterprising of the landowners achieve a fair competence and live in true New England comfort. The sons and daughters of Mt. Desert have honored their native island in various callings, by land and sea. The school-house at Hull's Cove was a gift from a retired sea-captain, well known in Maine, who was a child of the neighborhood. The villages at the harbors and at the head of the sound have, each, its church and regular Sunday service, and the traveler passes the ancient school-houses, at the corners where four ways meet, on the windy hill that overlooks the sea, or almost lost in the shadow of the wood. In most of the districts a long school is kept in the spring and early summer, and a short one in the fall, for the ways are too long and rough for the children in the winter.

To many of the people, the harvest of the sea is at once their revenue and their bane. So immediate and so abundant in its return, it draws the men away from their homes, and blinds them to any advantage to be gained by slower process. "Are they so very poor?" I asked, after some acquaintance with the interiors of the fishermen's houses where the worn faces of the women,—all traces of beauty so early lost,—told a sad tale of discomforts, of ill-cooked food, and needless exposure to storm and cold. "Not poor," was the answer of one who knew whereof she spoke ; "but they do not know how to live. The men are away two-thirds of the time, and do not mind what their homes are or how their womenkind get along. It is in the worst-looking houses that you can find the hard gold. We never knew what the fishermen did with their money till the war brought it out." If the truth were told, it might be that it is only some faint sparks of Yankeehood which keep some of these islanders from sinking quite to the level of "the Mucklebackits," whom a fellow-voyager suggested as the imaginative type of their class. Satisfied by the ease with which a bare subsistence is earned, they despise the wealth which the sea lays at their feet at every tide. Why till these stony fields, when "the land that no man ploughs" lies at my door ?—is the unconscious logic which overlooks or wastes the invaluable manures of the sea, and condemns to barrenness lands that else might blossom like a garden.

The preceding paragraph is no just description of the Island in 1885. It is retained as a record of a state of things now quite of the past here, and soon to disappear elsewhere in Maine, in the rapid transformation which is turning the long stretches of rocky sea-coast into summer resorts. The decline of the herring-fishery, and the gradual centering of other fishing interests in towns like Boothbay and Gloucester would have been an overwhelming loss to the Island, had not the influx of summer visitors provided new means of subsistence.

The change was slow at first, but the last six years have produced a marked improvement throughout the Island. The old houses have been repaired, new are built and farms and gardens show the thrift which the close vicinity of a good market inspires. It is worth while now to clear the forests away (as they are doing at the foot of Kebo and in Sawyer's Valley), when all the hay that can be raised finds a quick sale within an hour's drive. It is a fine proof of the power of adaptation in New England character that these people have thus taught themselves. Nearly all the hotels at Bar Harbor are in the hands of the families who lived in the half-dozen houses of the little hamlet of twenty years ago. Nor do the islanders show their better circumstances in their homes and their lands only. The school houses, notably in Eden, have been rebuilt, larger, brighter and far more attractive than the old.

Such is Mount Desert. The hurried traveler hastening from point to point, carries away a conception of only the grander, more awe-inspiring features of the

scene, and recalls them with a certain sense of breath-
lessness,—of holding on for one's life; but to him who
tarries longer there comes a perception of the picturesque
and tender elements which help to make up this rare
combination. Along the brooks are "sunny bits of
greenery," where one may lie and dream away a summer
holiday. Who that ever knew them, could forget the
quiet charm of the coves at the head of the sound; the
mill in the meadow under Kebo and the merry brook
below it; or the pebbly beach on the north side of Bar
Island; the long, bright bay beyond, and the soft ripple
of the waves, dying in harmony with the murmur of the
pines? Calm sunrises over quiet seas, broad moonlight
on shining forests, glowing sunsets across purpling distance, and tender afterglow on shadowy hills, complete
the radiant changes of the days. One would fain linger
till the autumnal breezes fill the air, and the October
splendor lights up the valleys. Late September is
likely to be most clear of fog, and one would be glad to
see the wonder of the equinoctial gale; but the days are
short and the dews are heavy. July will, perhaps, afford
all the requisites of good weather before the dog-days
begin. Even the fog is worth the watching, if one can
be reconciled to its disappointments. It lies off at sea
by day, drifts in at night or shifts with the tide, now
arches the valleys from peak to peak, now caps the

mountains, now folds them in softest fleeces, then rolls off in films of gossamer. It was after three weary days of fog, that I first found the Mount Desert of my dreams. Waking early, the rosy tint upon the curtain told of sunlit skies. Beneath my window, the harbor-bar lay moaning. On one black rock a white gull flapped his wings, while his comrades flew screaming past the dark cliffs of Bar Island. All along the shore the white spray glanced and glittered. The mountains stood blue and cold in the south, and seaward swept the fog in great masses like an army with banners.

One may always find goodly company at Mount Desert—wise men of affairs, accomplished men of letters, artists, students, fair women and bright girls; but I leave to fancy, the summer idyls, the romances by the sea.

In parting, I beg the reader to believe that I have always said less rather than more, in describing the only neighborhood of mountain and sea on all our Atlantic coast. These cliffs look down not on bay or lake, but upon broad ocean. It is to find in one the Isles of Shoals and Wachusett; or Nahant and Monadnock; Newport and the Catskills.

NOVEMBER, 1866.

EXCURSIONS FROM BAR HARBOR.

FIRST and nearest is the WALK, that is, the path along the shore from the steamboat-landing towards Cromwell's Harbor. Those who knew it long ago will regret the disappearance of the morning-glories and the harebells, but the views of bay and islands must always be fine. There are sheltered nooks for a morning's reading, and fanciful names have been given to many points along the walk,—the Pulpit, etc.; but as they vary with the enthusiasm of succeeding summers it is difficult to identify them.

The courtesy of private owners has more or less explicitly conceded the continuance of this walk,—for to bar the casual visitor from it would be a hardship. But it is a matter of the greatest importance and one upon which the Guide Book is bound to insist that this sacrifice of a certain amount of private right and private enjoyment should be met on the part of the public by a scrupulous regard for what is still reserved for personal ownership. If the walk is open for a stroll and the rocks accessible for resting places, all else should in return be considered as behind bolts and bars. No bathing or fishing should

be attempted, no foot stray upon the lawn inside the path and no least branch or flower be broken.

Over the Bar to the ISLAND when the tide serves is an inviting stroll. Visitors should ascertain before starting how long the Bar will be uncovered, lest they find it an awkward delay to wait for a boat to take them back. If the season is good and the weirs are in order, there is much of interest in watching the taking of fish out of them. From the height of the Island the village of Bar Harbor shows to the best advantage. The woods on the north side of the Island are a tempting resort for a warm summer afternoon, and the pebbly beach with the sunset view across the bay is just the place for a gypsy tea, all the more, that it is so near home.

The MILL IN THE MEADOW, near Mount Kebo, is a pleasant spot by a brown brook that ripples along under the shadows. The road is the second to the right leading from Kebo street and crosses the road to the race-course, almost losing itself across the fields edged with wild roses and blackberry vines.

To reach MOUNT KEBO take the same turn from Kebo St. and when three ways divide choose the middle, and then generally follow the best traveled one until three ways divide again. Then turn to the right and the path will be found on the left after a little distance. It is but a short climb and then will be found a surprising view of the village and the bay. No other point accessible shows so well the sweep and the slope of the lower hills. Standing in the village it may seem that all the best sites have been taken, but from this point it is evident that all along the circuit of Great Pond Hill, Kebo and Strawberry Hill, there are points not at all inconvenient of access and yet far more commanding than any yet occupied.

The distance to Duck Brook is trifling in the eyes of those enthusiastic pedestrians who have made Mount Desert their special field, but it is long enough to make the suggestion of driving as far as the bridge not out of place for those to whom either time or strength is precious. The real attraction of the walk is the ramble along the brook, sometimes on one side, sometimes on the other, and not seldom in the bed of the brook itself.

It has been a point of honor for ambitious climbers, to achieve the whole distance to the Mill on the Floss, where the Somesville road crosses the brook not far from its source at Eagle Lake. The "Mill on the Floss" was the huge frame of a half-built mill, which, after standing for many years, was pulled down in order to use the timber elsewhere. It was the most significant memento left of the old "lumbering" time in Mount Desert. What giants there were in those days, may be

4

learned from the moss-grown trunks that still lie along the banks of Duck Brook. In not a few places the remnants of the "ways" can be distinctly traced, by which the timber was brought down the hill-sides to the brook.

The POND OF WITCH HOLLOW lies to the left of the old road over Duck Brook Hill, and not far beyond the summit, so that it is a surprise to find so large a sheet of water at what seems so great a height. A wood-road descends rapidly to the shore which, like the low hills about the pond, is well covered with trees, making a very pretty sylvan scene.

At SANDS' POINT are the OVENS, by which general name the whole sea-coast population have always called those hollows which the action of the waves so frequently makes in the softer or more friable rocks. The road to the Point runs through the village at Hull's Cove, in which the only object of special interest to the traveler is the little cemetery on the hill, where are the "French Graves" (see page 63). A walking party will find it pleasant to leave the road here, keeping to the right across Point Levi and following the shore to the Ovens. The wagons would take the first well-traveled road to the right beyond the woods.

The Ovens have been renamed variously the Cloisters, the Via Mala, the Cathedral, etc.; but if one must have an architectural simile, they are really more like the

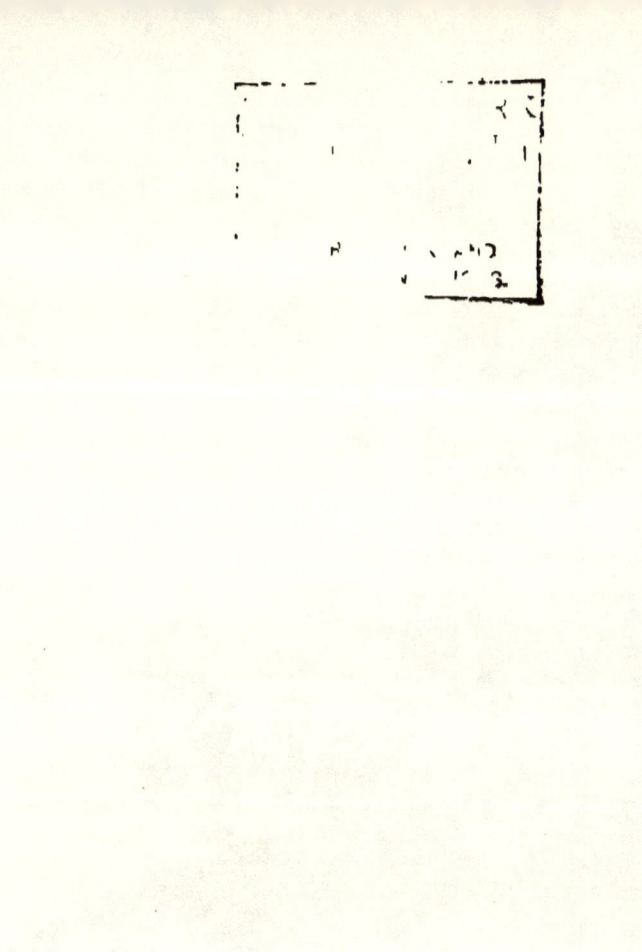

bold arches with zig-zag mouldings in the depths of which the old Romanesque builders placed there doorways. The Cathedral rock is on the right from the foot of the path and the Ovens on the left. They are quite hidden from sight at the top of the cliff, and can only be reached by land an hour or two from high tide. There is a gravel beach below them then, on which quaint picnic parties have been given, with the moon lighting the grim cliff behind, or the ruddy glow of bonfires flashing up under the dark arches. They are worth at least a double visit, one by land and one by water. At high tide the boats may pass directly under the larger arches. It is worth while to suggest that the shadows from the west increase the effect both of height and depth.

At SCHOONER HEAD and GREAT HEAD, three and four miles southeast of Bar Harbor, are the SPOUTING HORN, ANEMONE CAVE, and NEWPORT BEACH (see page 44). Tourists with little time to spare visit all these points in one day. The Cave can be entered only at low tide, and the cliffs at Great Head are more impressive at that hour, though the surf is higher at full tide or during the two hours preceding.

The drive to OTTER CLIFFS is through the GORGE (see page 42), the deep and narrow valley between Dry Mountain and Newport. The Cliffs form the eastern face of a bold headland which corresponds to Great

Head, the two inclosing a shallow bay with Newport Beach at the east, and the two finely-rounded hills, the Peak of Otter and the Bee-Hive, behind it.

On the other side of this headland lies Otter Creek Cove, repeating Somes' Sound on a tiny scale. The path to the cliffs leads to the right from the cottage where the wagons are left, through a beautiful piece of pine woods hung with gray moss and cushioned beneath with the softest green. In the wood is a bold cliff with the trees about it blasted by lightning, that makes a wild, solitary scene.

The Otter Cliffs themselves rise straight and sheer from the water one hundred and twelve feet, and bravely front the northeast winds that must toss the winter waves upon them with fearful force.

Another path from the house turns to the left, and following the shore towards Great Head brings one to THUNDER HOLE or THUNDER CAVE, a deep chasm into which with every returning wave the water rolls and swirls, and when wind and tide conspire, the wave is thrown against the overhanging rock with a blow that makes the whole cliff shake and the air tremble as with the crash of thunder. The wind should be south of east and the tide just at the point to throw the wave under the rock. Failing this there will be disappointment.

There is a path from the Otter Creek road to Newport

Beach that might be taken in returning. The wagons can go round to meet the party at the cottage near the beach.

THE TWENTY-TWO MILE DRIVE is the long circuit from Bar Harbor down through the Gorge by Otter Creek and Northeast Harbor.

The old road, so well remembered for its roughness, has been much improved and in some places wholly remade on a better line. After crossing the lower ridge of Pemetic there is a picturesque winding road to the north that takes one to Jordan's Pond (see page 38). Beyond, the main road crosses the Coves on the front of the island,—once, over the top of a sea-wall,—to Northeast harbor. It then turns northward, skirting the harbor. It leaves on the left the Hadlock Lower Pond and crosses the outlet of the Upper Pond very near the pond itself. It then passes close under the cliff of the Brown Mountain (about 700 feet high at the steepest point) through the pleasantest piece of woods on the Island. When it leaves the wood it is even then some two hundred feet above the level of the Sound. It descends gradually until it meets the Somesville Road near the head of Richardson's Cove. Thence the drive follows the straight road to Bar Harbor, which is just on the edge of the hill-country, so that it gives fine views of Sargent, the Twins, and Green Mountain, while no-

where else does Pemetic assert its individual self so
markedly as when seen near the road to Eagle Lake.
Its sharp, serrated edge stands clearly out against the
sky, stamping itself more strongly on the memory than
any outline of all the rest.

Such is the DRIVE. It need not take more than the
long half of a day, even when varied by a detour to
Jordan's Pond or Somesville. But the tourist who sees
it only thus has turned his back upon half its attractions. No road is known to one who has traversed it
only one way. Going up from Northeast Harbor one
misses much of the charm of the seaward view, or re-
versing it, one loses both there and on the Somesville
road the best sight of the hills. Only when seen across
Hadlock's Upper Pond does Sargent redeem the bold
promise it makes from the ocean. The great spurs
sweep round it like a magnificent amphitheatre.

Might the Guide Book suggest a better fashion of
making the excursion? Is it not worth dividing into two
for all but hurried travelers; and might not Northeast
Harbor be made the goal of both? Of all the little bays
and coves of this "nook-shotten isle," none is fairer than
this, with the smooth green fields and shaded slopes
around it.

Driving thither by the Gorge and Otter Creek, one
might spend an hour or two on the shore, or even eat a

picnic dinner in the shade; then returning, stop for a gypsy tea at Jordan's Pond just at that sunset hour when it shows its beauty most, and so home through the Gorge as it darkens with the evening shadows.

Then some other day going by the Somesville road, down the Sound by the Brown Mountain, a party might take the road that leads down the right shore of Northeast Harbor, and picnic on the slope that looks out across the Sound to Dog Mountain. (See page 99.) This would give the shorter half of the Drive, and there would be ample time for tea at the hospitable table of the Mount Desert House, in Somesville. The Guide Book ought to add, that he has not seen Mount Desert who has not seen the Sound at sunset.

The old road up GREEN MOUNTAIN has had a history and at present, (March, 1885), it may be said to have seen better days. As far back as 1850 there was a good road for ox-teams, constructed for the use of the officers of the Coast Survey who then had one of their principal stations upon the summit. In 1860 and '63 it had been so far washed out and overgrown as to be practicable for pedestrians only. Almost immediately after the steamboats began to run, a tolerable carriage road was made pretty much upon the line of the original one, and this was maintained in fair order until the summer of 1883. In the spring of that year a railroad was built upon the same plan as the well-known one upon Mount Washington. There is the same apparatus of cog-wheels and massive brakes, but unlike those roads there is no high trestle-work. Except for a few feet over a brook, the road bed is made throughout its entire length, of timber bolted directly on to the solid rock. This brings the body of the car very low and the motion, (it cannot be called speed) is so slow either going up or down that it is no exaggeration to say that a person accustomed to jump upon the horse-cars, could easily and safely step on or off at pleasure. The grade is about one foot in four and a half. Naturally the shortest route from summit to base was chosen. It is much to the west of the old road which followed the long ridge of Great Hill, and it descends to the head of Eagle Lake.

Passengers are carried in barges from Bar Harbor to the Lake and thence by the stern-wheel steamer, Wauwinet to the railroad station. It takes twenty minutes to cross the lake and about twenty-five to ascend the mountain. In connection with the railroad a most comfortable and tastefully appointed house[1] was built. A party of twenty or thirty would find themselves almost luxuriously accommodated for a night, and even a trav-

---

[1]The reluctant eyes of the passengers from Mount Desert Ferry to Bar Harbor in the bright moonlight of the evening of Aug. 2, 1884 saw the total destruction of this house by fire. At this writing (March, 1885) a still larger one is about to be built on the ledge directly overlooking Bar Harbor Village.

cler here alone would be re-paid by the impressive silence
of the solitude upon this great watch-tower above the sea.
In either case, the many or the one, let a night upon
the mountain be the one thing not to be missed in a visit
to Mount Desert.

The carriage road still exists and though its future as
such, may be uncertain, it is likely to be maintained as a
bridle and a footpath. After the novelty of the railway
is past, the road will be again frequented if not for the
whole ascent, at least as far as the ledge overlooking
Eagle Lake, for the sake of the western view, and there
gray-haired wisdom may tell ingenuous youth of the sunsets of long ago. It is not too far to Bar Harbor for a
walk back in a summer twilight.

The view from the top has been already described
in the general sketch of the Island (see page 40).

Youth and enthusiasm are wont to find scope for their
ambition, in the descent of Green Mountain, by way
of the deep ravine that separates it from Dry Mountain;
thence along the cliffs on the west side of the Gorge;
and so down into the upper end of the Gorge, or nearer
Kebo, out by the Mill in the Meadow. A less difficult, though a longer walk, is down the slope to Otter
Creek. This route has the advantage of the ocean
view. It is needless to say that there are fine oppor-
tunities for being lost on either walk, but it may be a

useful hint to add that the one thing 'to do in such a
case is to turn resolutely upward till some well-known
point is found. Bearing this in mind, no one need be
lost at Mount Desert anywhere for more than an hour
or two.

It was the fashion to speak slightingly of NEWPORT
MOUNTAIN in comparison with its loftier neighbor, but
in fact the lesser height and the nearness to the shore
and the sea, add a picturesque element which greatly
increases the charm of the view and more than com-
pensates for the loss in extent. The road to the mountain turns to the left from the Otter Creek road, not
far beyond where the latter leaves the one to Schooner
Head. The path ascends very gradually through the
woods to the ledges, across which it is marked by little
heaps of stones. Their position should be carefully
noticed, as the path may be missed on the bare rock.
The top is rather a long, flat ridge than a summit, and
the walk along the edge overlooking Schooner Head
almost gives the sensation of a flight in mid-air. A whole
day is as well spent in this excursion as in that to Green
Mountain. Resting in some sheltered nook at the outer
end of the ridge, one will find a long summer's day all
too short to watch the wonderful changing lights of sea
and sky. Go early enough to see the ocean glittering
like a pavement of burnished steel under a dome of sap-

phire, and wait for the tender, faint shadows of the wan-
ing afternoon to deepen into the dusky purple tints of
the sunset.   To the lovers of a tough scramble is commended a descent through the woods to Newport Beach,
but care should be taken to start early.

PEMETIC is at present beyond the reach of ladies.   It
is a long, hard climb to the top, from Jordan's Pond,
and a better way to it is by boat up Eagle Lake to the
sand beach at the head.   Here may be found what little
remains of the old forest on the Island.   Through this
the ascent is slow on account of the fallen timber, but it
is perfectly practicable and need not take above two
hours.   The view might be considered finer than that
from Green Mountain, from its nearness to the many
islands lying southwest; but this is even more true of
that from Dog Mountain or Western which are much
easier to reach.   The chief contribution of Pemetic to
the attractions of the Island is its sharp outline when
seen either from the north or south.

Within the last three years, the roads have been so
greatly improved and so many new ones made that there
are now a number of "circular drives" of great interest.
To no part of Maine has the enforcement of the fencing
laws, (that is allowing no cattle to run at large) been of
greater importance than at Mount Desert.   The tender
young growth which used to be constantly cropped back

by the cattle now makes a fresh and beautiful border
for the roads.

The great drive is of course round the whole Island
with the Narrows and Bass Harbor Head for the extreme
northern and southern points. It could be done in one
day by starting early and changing horses, but it would
be better to stop one night at least. This could be done
comfortably at Bass Harbor.

Of short drives, the one along the new road on the
shore of Frenchman's Bay is the finest. The return
may be made over the old road down Cork Screw Hill.
Another circuit is by the same road to Hull's Cove and
thence to the Eagle Lake road by Breakneck which is
now only a *lucus a non*. Or, take the first left-hand
road beyond Hull's Cove and cross to Town Hill and
back by Somesville. Again, keep on to Salisbury's
Cove, turn directly south, take either of the two roads
as they will unite before reaching McFarland's Mt. (see
map). The longer is the Norway Drive through young
but pretty woods. It is the most varied of all the wood-
land drives. It can be made longer by driving west to
Town Hill and again back by Somesville. Quite up to
the Narrows and back by Town Hill and Somesville, or
to shorten it by crossing to the Norway Drive, makes a
fine excursion for an afternoon. It is nearly as far as
to Northeast Harbor but not quite so fatiguing.

The new ·road about to be built between Sawyer's
Valley (the little settlement high up on the east of
Eagle Lake which is visible from all points overlooking
the Lake) out to the Somesville road at McFarland's
Mountain, will soon be followed by a short one from the
Valley to Jordan's Pond thus opening two circuits besides
a new way to North East Harbor.

Two other roads are to be made sooner or later. One
from Newport Beach to Otter Cliffs will open a circular
drive through the Gorge and back by Schooner Head.
Another from Otter Creek along the shore by the Stony
Beach would give the ocean views which are shut off
from the Twenty-two Mile Drive.

Boating is naturally a favorite amusement at Bar Harbor. Nothing marks more strongly the contrast between
the old time and the new than the fleet of trim row-boats
at the landing. There are good boats, too, on Eagle
Lake, and a gypsy tea on the beach at the upper end is
a frequent entertainment. Yet some one ought to give
a word of caution. Two or three accidents, one at least
fatal in the early time, enforced care and prudence about
sailing or rowing on the Bay. Not so at Eagle Lake,
where it is much to be feared that the boats are often
overcrowded with inexperienced persons. The boatmen
there are to be trusted, and should be consulted and
then obeyed.

There is a pretty and easy walk from the extreme southeast of Eagle Lake to Turtle Lake close under both Green and Pemetic. The walk to Jordan's Pond is a scramble, but not a very long one. The path is to the west leaving Pemetic on the left. A signal will be found at the head of the pond by which a boat to cross it can be obtained.

This completes the group of excursions of which Bar Harbor may be termed the centre. There is, in fact, no part of the Island which is not easily accessible thence in one day, but the objects of interest at the Sound and to the west of it naturally group themselves round Somesville and Southwest Harbor.

The two steamboats now afford a less hazardous, though a less romantic trip, to Southwest Harbor than the old sail-boats. The circuit from Bar Harbor to Southwest and back by way of Somesville is often made. The buck-boards are now often carried by the steamboat with the party. The return offers the choice of driving all the way back, or of rowing up the Sound (see page 37) and driving only from Somesville.

If there is only time to go once to Southwest Harbor, this trip may include a visit to Saint Sauveur by landing in Valley Cove (see page 59); or time may be saved by ordering the boats to wait there and driving up to meet them. Orders can be sent by telegraph.

It has been usual to make this trip by the Portland boat and row up the Sound : but the reverse, that is, the rowing from the heart of the Island through the mountains down to the open sea, will be found more impressive. It can be done in time to return by boat from Southwest Harbor in the afternoon. Indeed, it is worth the doing, independent of the outside voyage, even if one must return by the road.

The Guide Book can hardly enumerate all the combinations of this sort that are possible. To row down the Sound, touching at the foot of Dog Mountain, and landing at Manchester's near Northeast Harbor, is one of the best. The buck-boards that take the party to Somesville could then meet it at the Harbor.

EXCURSIONS FROM SOMESVILLE.

In old times, Somesville, with a stage and a mail twice a week, even in winter, was on the high-road of travel, but it is now quite left to itself, except for a merry dinner or tea-party at one of the hotels.

The little village deserves much greater consideration. It is within easy reach of all points of interest, and its very want of sea view will be in a way its special attraction, for it is really a village some five or six miles *inland*, and its climate is materially affected by its position as compared with either of the harbors. The sharpness and chill of the sea air are perceptibly softened, making it for many persons a much safer and more agreeable resort than the open shore.

Often when all the harbors are shrouded in fog, the day is bright and clear and the southerly wind brings up hour after hour the doleful sound of the fog-horn at the light-house.

The SARGENT MOUNTAIN is usually ascended from Somesville by crossing the Sound and landing near the brook at the mouth of Sargent's Cove. The wood roads once existing have been pretty much overgrown, so that there is no regular path.   It is a long, hard climb, and would repay only those who want the walk for its own sake.   The summit is too far from the sea or the Sound, and the landscape too much hidden by the great spurs to make the view equal to that from Green Mountain. What is most remarkable about Sargent is these great spurs, or shoulders, nine hundred and a thousand feet high which make it rather a group of peaks than a single mountain.   Eagle Lake, Jordan's Pond, and the Had-lock Ponds, lie close under them, and the view down into them from the overhanging precipices is said to be well worth the labor of the long circuit of the mountain sides. (See 98).

The path from the Brown Farm up the Brown Moun-tain which overlooks the Sound is well-trodden for thither go the blueberry pickers sure to find the finest on the top.   The view repays the trouble of the ascent.   Some visitors say, "go up Brown if nowhere else."

Most of the Bar Harbor "circular drives" are not too long if taken from Somesville and those to the north and west of the village are likewise within reach of Bar Har-bor.   The best after that through the mountains, is west across Pretty Marsh round to Indian Point Village, thence back by Oak Hill, or farther by Town Hill.   It should be taken in this order for the sake of the grand view of the mountains from Indian Point Village.   The tide should be high to fill the numerous coves. High Head is a noble bluff equal to Great Head except that it looks upon inland and quiet waters. Time should be allowed to walk up to it from the road. It overlooks Bluehill Bay.

The four points of view not on the mountains which surpass all others may be selected as Great Head, Bass Harbor Head, High Head, and Indian Point Village.

The road on Beech Hill Ridge is part of an ancient highway long since discontinued beyond the Carter Farm. It was the regular route between Somesville and Southwest Harbor until the shorter road by Deming's Pond was laid out. Abandoned as it is, it is not even now impassable for light vehicles. The bare ledges that made it in the old time very unsafe in winter, for about a hundred yards, near the beginning of the descent towards Southwest Harbor, are the only places that are at all difficult. The rest of the way is a series of delightful surprises. Overarched and embowered by the growth of thirty years, the road itself is clear and smooth, and covered by close green grass which, where it is walled in by tall rows of arbor-vitæ, makes it seem more like the soft turf walks of a well-trimmed garden, than like a neglected bit of country-side.

It leads through the CARTER NOTCH to a sudden outlook down upon Southwest Harbor, with the islands and the ocean beyond, a scene as beautiful as it is unexpected. A deep ravine borders the road here, and beyond it the mountain rises in a steep palisade. It would be a rough rather than a difficult climb to scale it, and beyond is no doubt a fine view of Long Pond.

This Notch road comes out at Norwood's Cove, near Fernald's Point. It is here made known, with some misgiving, lest the attempt to make a drive of the excursion should, in one summer, rob it of its special charm. Let it be preserved for a *walk*. It is by no means too long, especially if the wagons for the return are sent down the main road to Norwood's Cove.

When our exploring party came through from Southwest Harbor last summer (1876), old Mr. Carter's salutation, as we drew up at his door, was, "You are the first woman through there for twenty years." The day before he had completely denied the possibility of doing it. Telling our adventures to the kindly hostess of the Mount Desert House, at Somesville, she averred, "It is *twenty-five* years since any woman went through. The last time I went down that way, was when I drove down to bring back my husband, after he had chained out the new road by the Pond. That was thirty-two years ago."

In point of fact, no spring-vehicle had ever gone over the road before, for not a single one was on the Island before the road was discontinued. It was an odd coincidence, that the light wagon in which we had driven was the first with springs ever brought on to the Island.

Our hostess gave us a further bit of local history. "My husband brought *the first horse* to the Island forty-two years ago."

This account of the road is preserved like some other pages of the Guide Book as a momento of things that were. The road has been remade from the point where the Sand Cove road crosses it, and while the loss of the old charm is to be regretted by the pedestrian, the drive is now enjoyed by the hundreds who take it as one half of a circuit including Somesville and Southwest Harbor. It is best to take the mountain road southward, going or coming northward by the shore of the pond.

From the Carter Farm two short walks can be taken which will repay the tourist; one to the CARTER'S NUB-BLE, which overlooks the farm, and commands the western view; the other on the left, to the top of ECHO CLIFF, on the shore of Deming's Pond. This point is the end of what is known at Bar Harbor as the BEECH HILL DRIVE. The cliff itself and the view are like Dog Mountain on a smaller scale.

The three ponds that lie west of the Sound are within a circuit made by the road west from Somesville to the foot of LONG POND; thence across the rolling country to the head of Seal Cove Pond which is very near the seashore. This pond lies just under the side of the Western Mountain. It empties into Seal Cove, which, with its high banks and narrow outlet, makes the most picturesque scene on the western coast. The cross-road to the left should be taken just after passing the bridge. This crosses the Island directly to Norwood's Cove on Somes' Sound; thence, turning to the left, the road to Somesville is followed with Dog Mountain and Robinson's on the right and Deming's Pond on the left. Across the pond is ECHO CLIFF, a precipice four hundred feet high.

Pleasant as this drive is, it fails to give any adequate view of LONG POND. To know how beautiful that is, one must go by the road along the top of Beech Hill Ridge, which commands a fine western prospect, and across the fields to the slope of the hill. The pond lies in a long valley between the Western Mountain and Beach Mountain, whose beautiful forest-covered slopes rise gently round it, giving to the landscape a serene aspect that contrasts agreeably with the barren cliffs along the Sound. (See page 106.)

There is a large quarry on the west shore of the sound, but the village belonging to it is entirely hidden both from the water and the highway. It is large enough for a school of its own with thirty or more children. A granite quarry is by no means a novel sight, but the rock is seldom seen in great sheets like these lying one above the other on the slope towards the water.

There is a tempting opportunity for a very rough scramble through the high valley between Robinson's Mountain and Dog. Leave the high-road when a little above the north end of the Echo Cliff opposite, and, keeping near the steep rocks on the left, cross the ridge and descend to the shore of the Sound by the bed of the Man-of-war Brook. The Gold Digger's Glen is near by.

To reach Dog Mountain from Somesville, follow the Southwest Harbor road for about three quarters of a mile below Deming's Pond, then through the bars at the left to the little cottage under the mountain. The ascent may be made in half an hour, and is so easy that there is hardly any regular path. Keep straight up behind the cottage over the first pitch, then gradually to the left till the summit shows itself. Another ascent can be made from the shore of the Sound. There is a rough pasture covered with bluebells at the foot of the mountain. The beach under the cliff is bordered at low tide with urchins and star fish. No better place could be found to show to children the crowded life of sea creatures.

Many visitors have felt this view more impressive than anything else at Mount Desert. After a mountain walk, so easy as to be commonplace, one suddenly finds one's self on the brink of Eagle Cliff, a precipice that falls sheer down hundreds of feet to the dark water below. More even than Newport Cliffs, it gives the sense of being poised in mid-air. Like them its nearness to the water gives an effect of height far beyond the actual one.

A visit to Northeast Harbor, though easily made a part of the Twenty-two mile Drive (see page 77,) properly belongs to the group of Somesville excursions.[1]

<hr>

[1]The railroad company now sends a steamboat at least once a day to Northeast Harbor so that connection is sure and easy with Mount Desert Ferry. The same boat calls at Seal Harbor.

The Harbor has been already mentioned as the most picturesque and attractive in itself of all the harbors. There are hotels and boarding-houses as comfortable as anything at Bar Harbor while there is more of the old quiet and of the old freedom of life. The little chapel of St. Mary's by the Sea is at the top of the rise from the steamboat landing on the west side. A path has been made, or more exactly, marked out by blazing and by painting red arrows, to the top of Sargent, and since the old wood roads are now so overgrown, it is much the easiest way to ascend the mountain. There is a similar path hardly two miles long through the woods to Jordan's Pond. Asticou, the hill on the east side of the head of the harbor is as fortunately placed for a view from it as Kebo at Bar Harbor. The ascent is very easy as this path is also marked by arrows and blazing. The slowest walker would do it in an hour. For beauty of landscape, sunset is the proper time. To see the western view clearly the morning hours should be chosen. The Isle au Haut is in a line with Greening's Island and the southeast point of the shore of Southwest Harbor.

The broad promontory which separates the Harbor from Somes' Sound commands beautiful views of the islands on all sides ; the finest, however, is from a point well up the Sound, about two miles above Southwest Harbor. To reach this point from Somesville, take the right hand road at the head of the Harbor. It runs at first high up on the western shore, then rounds the southern spur of the Brown Mountain and turns to the north. One must go quite to the end of the road at a solitary little farm-house. The left hand road (after turning north) leads only to the lower shore of the promontory, a *détour* worth making on the return, but not to be mistaken for the real object of the excursion,—the view up and across the Sound.

The Corson Farm slopes smooth and green to the water's edge. Right opposite are the steep cliffs of Dog Mountain, and deep in their shadow, Valley Cove. The Robinson Mountain shows here, and only here, as it does from the Sound, its long level crest against the sky, and northward stretch the placid waters of the Sound. Coming suddenly out of the woods into sight of this landscape it is something such a revelation as the reverse of this very picture, the view from the top of Dog Mountain.

The road through the woods has been closed up so that there is now no choice for carriages but to take the lower and longer one. The old one is still available for a walk, thus making an interesting and not overlong circuit from the Harbor. The Manchester place, where the great shell-heaps are, is on the north-west side of Sandy Cove. The road passes close to the top of the shell bank.

This excursion cannot be too strongly commended to those who are prevented, by want of time or foggy weather, from rowing up or down the Sound itself. (See page 37.) It as nearly as possible replaces the latter.

A visit to this spot, in 1876, will be long remembered for the wonderful effect of haze and smoke from distant forest fires, in the soft atmosphere of early September. In it the mountains seemed to recede and lie far away and dim. It added to the landscape that last charm which we sometimes miss at Mount Desert—the glamour of distance.

EXCURSIONS FROM SOUTHWEST HARBOR.

ALL the west of the Island is as easily reached from Southwest Harbor as from Somesville.

DOG MOUNTAIN may be ascended by taking the road to Fernald's Point and leaving it near the head of Norwood's Cove. There is a wood road that leads thence to the cottage under the mountain mentioned in the Somesville excursions, but the climb right up from the Cove is not very difficult, and it affords fine views of the Sound and of the face of Eagle Cliff. (See page 37.) The same walk might include the reputed site of the SAINT SAVEUR Colony (see page 59), or that may be visited on the way to the FLYING MOUNTAIN, the low conical hill that stands like a sturdy little warden at the gateway of the Sound. Its curious position makes it a kind of central point for views of the most varied kinds, and some of the most beautiful landscapes, uniting mountain and sea, to be found at the Island, are here.

All passengers on the steamboats will remember the low light-house beneath the bluff at Bass Harbor Head. From the bluff itself there is a superb panoramic view only surpassed by that from Green Mountain. For the hills it is very nearly the reverse of that seen from the high land in coming down from Bangor. Good walkers would prefer to reach the Head by way of the sea-wall (see page 53), from which it is about three miles distant by the shore. To drive—follow the main road to the right. The lowland which forms the southern extremity of the Island is more varied and more picturesque than that at the north. The road has not a few sudden surprises as it winds its way to the high stony ridge which leads from the head of Bass Harbor to the Light. Sunset is the hour to be there. All along the north stretch the hills from faint Schoodic to fainter Bluehill in the golden haze of the west, while opposite are the ocean itself and the wide sweep of the land-locked bay. Close at hand glitter the many coves of the much indented shore. It is worth repeating. It is all that is finest, most wonderful at Mount Desert, after Green Mountain.

So much was said in 1880. The change in the direction of travel, by which comparatively few people will now come to Bar Harbor by sea, gives a vastly greater importance to this view. No one can afford to leave it out of a visit to Mount Desert. Though the distance is long, it is nothing like the undertaking it used to be to take the twenty-two mile drive over the old rough roads.

It will not be long before people will come to stay a night at Bass Harbor for the sake of the sunset at the Head.

The unique possession of Southwest Harbor is the drive to the WHITE BEACH. It is not too far for a drive from Bar Harbor, but hitherto it has been seldom visited by the company there. The name is an obvious suggestion of the sea-shore, so that it is another of the surprises which so varied a landscape as that of Mount Desert continually offers, to see the horses' heads turned away from the sea.

The Somesville road is left just below Norwood's Cove and the Seal Cove road followed for about two thirds of a mile, then turn again northward and enter an old wood-road, one of those "ribbon roads" so fascinating to children. It winds on and on through a thick grove of young trees, in which evergreens and birches are curiously intermingled. Keeping always to the right,[1] we descend at last by a sudden pitch, and find ourselves without warning on the WHITE BEACH, at the head of Long Pond.

No other scene upon the Island unites so many of the characteristic charms of *lake* scenery. (Jordan's Pond belongs rather to the mountains.) At either end of the

---

[1] That on the left, in a little clearing, leads to the site of the old mill. (See page 45.)

beach the Western Mountain and the Carter rise abruptly throwing long shadows across the water. These mountains are still covered with forest, as well as the whole shore of the pond,—when seen from this point, a circuit of some six or eight miles,—so that there is no sight of human habitation, nor sign of the hand of man. It is very still, very remote, but the vivid coloring of forest and lake, the softness and grace of outline in the whole landscape, give it a tender charm, which makes it a solitude of repose and rest, not of loneliness.

BEECH HILL and ECHO CLIFF (see page 93) are not too distant for a walk by the old road.

But the special claim of Southwest Harbor upon the tourist lies in the attractions of the Sound and the ocean itself. The many islands lying within easy distance afford great variety of interest for yachting parties. The winds are steadier than in Frenchman's Bay, making sailing less hazardous and plans for picnics less uncertain.

This is the best point from which to undertake the trip to MOUNT DESERT ROCK. Throughout the summer there is constant communication with the light-keeper, and for parties who can wait for clear weather, the trip can be easily arranged.

There is a regular ferry to the CRANBERRY ISLANDS. Tourists will soon find out what artists have long known, that some of the finest views of the hills are to be had

from them. Even a stay of a night there is to be recom
mended for the sake of the sunset and the sunrise on the
hills. Like their kindred, the Camden Hills, they sometimes take on a wonderful purple tint, not the cold, dark
hue we see on mountains inland, but with a roseate light
beneath as if illumined by a glow within.

Boating at the head of Somes' Sound has a charm all
its own (see page 37), but one must sail up as well as
down, to see fully the wild grandeur of this mountain
fiord.

At the entrance on the west are the green slopes of
Fernald's Point, and the Flying Mountain; then Eagle
Cliff (the eastern face of Dog Mountain). The Man-of-
War Brook comes down the high valley between Dog
Mountain and Robinson's. The bluff close above it is
known as the Crow's Nest. It makes one side of the
Narrows, and is nearly six hundred feet high. The
Brown Mountain on the other side is quite four hundred
feet high close to the Sound, though its greatest height
(eight hundred and eighty feet) is some distance east
at the cliff by Hadlock's Pond. Above the Narrows
the Sound widens and the mountains recede, the bare
rugged sides of Sargent throwing into strongest contrast
the smooth fields round the little village of Somesville,
which forms the terminus of the voyage.

HOW TO MAKE THE BEST USE OF A SHORT VISIT.

THOSE fortunate persons who have a month or more to spend at Mount Desert, and can make the excursions at leisure, with the suggestions of those yet happier people who are all-summer residents, do not need the help of the Guide Book. To the hurried traveler, it is of the last importance to do only that which is best worth doing. The following hints are therefore offered for his benefit.

If the day be clear, the ascent of Green Mountain should be the first excursion of all, for no other so completely reveals the wonder of the island in the combination of mountain and sea.

Schooner Head and Great Head have always borne the palm as the finest points on the shore; but something of their pre-eminence may be due to the fact that in all the early time when horses were almost unknown, these two Heads were not too distant for a walk. Now they must divide the honors with Thunder Hole and Otter Cliffs, which lie farther to the southwest near Otter Creek Cove.

On a long July day, a party can drive to Schooner

Head, see the Spouting Horn and Anemone Cave,—perhaps dine there,—then, sending the horses round by the road, follow the path through the woods to Otter Creek, and visit Thunder Hole and the Cliffs. The drive home would show the Gorge just after sunset, when it is very impressive.

A day of fog need not interfere with this excursion, except the walk through the woods, and if there come a real storm with low driving clouds and a heavy surf, the expedition would repay a good deal of exposure to wind and rain. The traveler from far inland will take away a much more vivid sense of the grandeur of the ocean from such a day, than from one of sunshine alone.

The drive to Bass Harbor Head should take precedence of everything but the ascent of the mountain to those who have come by rail. The roads of the Twenty-two Mile Drive are now much more shut in by woods than they used to be, so that the drive is far more like any country drive.

The fourth day could be given to this, and it should be made to include the *détour* to the Corson Farm, near Northeast Harbor (see page 99), for only this view can at a single visit show what Somes' Sound is. Or if one prefers to look *over* the Sound rather than across it,—from the eagle's point of view, as it were,—it is possible to combine the Drive and the ascent of Dog Mountain in one expedition, though this is not to be recommended to any one who has two separate days to devote to them.

It was once made by two ladies with perfect ease, leaving Bar Harbor at 9 A. M., and returning at twenty minutes before seven P. M. They drove first through the Gorge to Jordan's Pond, spent a half an hour at the shore, then on to Somesville to dinner. The ascent of Dog Mountain took about two hours and a half. The road thither passes close to Deming's Pond, giving a fine view of the Echo Cliff. It may be well to add that to make so long a jaunt with comfort the wagons ought not to be filled as for Great Head. Six for each ought to be enough. It is also worth while to order beforehand the dinner at Somesville.

If two such long drives are too fatiguing a fourth day may be given to a visit to the Ovens returning by Salisbury Cove and the Norway Drive. This would require but half the day, so that the ascent of Newport could also be made.

These four days would thus give a visit to the most remarkable places on the Island, but the plan is by no means recommended to any one who has time to enjoy them at leisure.

CHURCHES AT BAR HARBOR.

———

THE ORTHODOX CONGREGATIONAL; the old church of
   East Eden.

SAINT SAVIOUR'S,   -   -   -   EPISCOPAL.

CLARK MEMORIAL,   -   -   METHODIST.

SAINT SYLVIA'S,   -   -   -   ROMAN CATHOLIC.

THE GAME LAWS OF MAINE.

The dates mark the limits of the seasons in which it is lawful to kill the game named:

Moose, deer and caribou, Oct. 1—Jan. 1 (forbidden to hunt with dogs), unlawful for one person to take more than one moose, two caribou and three deer (in one season); mink, beaver, sable, otter. fisher, muskrat, Oct. 15—May 1.

Wood-duck, dusky, black or other sea duck, Sept. 1—May 1; ruffed grouse (partridge), woodcock, Sept. 1—Dec. 1; pinnated grouse. Sept. 1—Jan. 1; plover, Aug. 1—May 1. Woodcock, ruffed grouse and plover may be killed only for consumption within the State. Sunday shooting forbidden. Wildfowl law does not apply to sea-coast.

Salmon, July 15, tide water—Sept. 15, with rod and line; smelts, April 1—Oct. 1; land-locked salmon, trout, togue, May 1—Oct. 1; black bass, Oswego bass, white perch, July 1—April 1.

Angling for salmon within one hundred yards of fish-way, dam or mill race, forbidden. Season for land-locked salmon, trout, togue, in St. Croix river and tributaries, and all waters in Kennebec County, May 1 to Sept. 15.

During months of February, March and April it is lawful for citizens to take land-locked salmon, trout, togue, "and convey the same to their homes, but not otherwise."

It is unlawful to take land-locked salmon less than nine (9) inches in length, or trout less than five (5) inches; or take, transport or have in possession for transportation more than fifty pounds of land-locked salmon, trout or togue, in all. Unlawful to take these fish in Kennebago, Mollychunkamunk, Cupsuptic, Mooselucmaguntic, and Welokennebacook Lakes and tributaries, between Feb. 1 and May 1; unlawful in said waters to use spawn bait in September.

It is unlawful to take trout or land-locked salmon in the Misery or Sacatien rivers, Moosehead Lake, from 10th Sept. to 1st May, or in the Rangeley stream, between the mouth of Kennebago stream and Howard's Dam, from July 1 to May 1; or at the South Bog stream, from July 1 to May 1: or in the Bemis stream, from July 1 to May 1: or the Cupsuptic stream, from July 1 to May 1; or in the Kennebago stream between the foot of the first falls, near its junction with the Rangeley stream, and the upper falls at the outlet of Kennebago Lake, from Sept. 1 to May 1; or Misery or Sacatien rivers, Moosehead Lake, from 10th September to 1st of May.

COMMISSIONERS:

E. M. STILLWELL, Bangor, } *Fisheries and Game.*
H. O. STANLEY, Dixfield, }

B. W. COUNCE, Thomaston, } *Sea and Shore Fisheries.*

···➤THE➤···

MAINE CENTRAL RAILROAD

**Extends from PORTLAND to and beyond Bangor, to the
BOUNDARY LINE between the State of Maine
and the Province of New Brunswick,**

UNITES THE RAILROADS OF THE UNITED STATES

———AND———

MARITIME PROVINCES,

**Forms with its own Lines, Branches and
Connections, the**

➤⁜ONLY RAIL ROUTE⁜◄

TO AND FROM

MOUNT DESERT

**And all parts of the STATE OF MAINE, and the
Provinces of**

New Brunswick and Nova Scotia,

**CAPE BRETON and PRINCE EDWARD ISLAND.
Best Route to**

Moosehead and the Rangeley Lakes,

**And all of the Noted Hunting and Fishing Resorts of Northern
Maine and New Brunswick; and leads to all the other Sea-
side Resorts to be found on the long line of Sea Coast
with which Maine and the Provinces abound.**

☞Through Tickets for all points reached by its Lines on sale at
nearly all the Ticket Offices throughout the country.

**ARTHUR SEWALL, President.   PAYSON TUCKER, Gen. Manager.
F. E. BOOTHBY, Gen. Passenger Agent.**

PORTLAND, ME.

PORTLAND, BANGOR, MT. DESERT AND MACHIAS
STEAMBOAT COMPANY.

THE DIRECT INSIDE LINE TO

MOUNT DESERT

IN CONNECTION WITH THE

BOSTON & MAINE and MAINE CENTRAL RAILROADS.

DURING THE SUMMER SEASON STEAMERS

Will leave Portland every Tuesday and Friday at 11.00 P. M., or on arrival of trains leaving Boston at 7.00 P. M., for **ROCKLAND, CASTINE, DEER ISLE,**

SOUTH WEST & BAR HARBORS,

MILLBRIDGE, JONESPORT AND MACHIASPORT.

Passengers for points East of Bar Harbor can also procure tickets for 7.00 P. M. train from Boston, on Tuesdays and Fridays, via All Rail Line to Bar Harbor, and take Steamer there.

Passengers by Rail to Rockland take day trains and remain in Rockland over night, taking Steamer Wednesday and Saturday mornings.

RETURNING :

Leave Machiasport every Monday and Thursday at 4.00 A. M., touching at Jonesport and Millbridge, and connecting at Mt. Desert Ferry with trains of Maine Central R. R., thence proceeding to Portland.

LEAVING BAR HARBOR ABOUT 10.00 A. M.,

Mondays and Thursdays, touching at all landings, arriving in Portland at 1.00 A. M., Tuesdays and Fridays, connecting with Pullman night train for Boston and the West.

Passengers wishing to take Later Trains will not be disturbed.

NOTE. Steamers run to Mt. Desert Ferry on Western Trip only. Passengers by rail to points reached by the Steamer on Eastward Trip will take Ferry Boat to Bar Harbor, and connect there.

Tickets for sale at principal stations on Boston & Maine and Maine Central Railroads and throughout the country. State rooms can be procured on board Steamers, and at 306 Washington Street, Boston, or on application to the General Passenger Agent.

The Direct Route between Boston, Portland, and all points on the Coast of Maine.

F. E. BOOTHBY,
General Pass. Agent.

PAYSON TUCKER,
General Manager.

Boston & Maine Railroad.

SEA SHORE LINE
— TO —

LAKE WINNEPESAUKEE,

THE WHITE MOUNTAINS!

And all the Pleasure Resorts in

NORTHERN NEW HAMPSHIRE,

THE STATE OF MAINE,

AND THE

EASTERN PROVINCES!

Special facilities afforded Tourists and Sportsmen visiting the

RANGELEY LAKES,

THE DEAD RIVER REGION, OR MOOSEHEAD LAKE.

THROUGH TRAINS TO

✳ MOUNT ✳ DESERT ✳

Send for "Summer Excursion Rates" and "Hotel and Boarding House List."

JAMES T. FURBER,
General Manager.

D. J. FLANDERS,
Gen. Pass. & Tkt. Agt.

ISLAND HOUSE,

SOUTH WEST HARBOR, MAINE.

THIS House is situated at South West Harbor, Mt. Desert Island, Maine, being on the South side of the Island, facing the Ocean, with the entire range of Mountains, 13 in number, in the shape of a half circle, in the background, with Somes' Sound, and a string of beautiful Islands which forms the Harbor, and makes a beautiful Bay of 5 miles in width, perfectly land-locked and safe for rowing or sailing parties, and is one of the most beautiful sheets of water about the Island. VALLEY COVE, 2 miles distant, on Somes' Sound, has the steepest cliffs and boldest scenery on the Island. LONG LAKE, a fresh water pond, between two high mountains, is a beautiful place two and one-half miles from the House, and will be supplied with row boats for use. ECHO LAKE is a place of much interest, and the sea wall, 3 miles south, is a wonderful formation. CRANBERRY BEACHES and DUCK ISLANDS are very pleasant places to visit. The roads are very good, and there are many fine drives, taking in Sea Wall, Bass Harbor Head, Goose Cove, Seal Cove, Pretty Marsh, Indian Point, Oak Hill, Seal Cove Pond, Cape High Head, a fine view of Blue Hill Bay, and returning over Beech Hill you have a fine view of the North Bays and main land, and descending Beech Mountain by carriage road you have a fine view of the main, ocean and islands surrounding South West Harbor. Privileges for Fishing, Sailing and Riding are unsurpassed by anything on or about the Island, and only need to be seen to be admired, and those in search of pleasure, rest or health will do well to visit South West Harbor.

The houses here are very comfortable, and price of board very moderate. South West Harbor and vicinity has fourteen hotels. The "Island House," the largest of them, can accommodate 150 guests, and has the most commanding location of any on the Island, is only a few rods from Steamer's landing, and has a wharf and slips purposely for Pleasure Boats, with a plank walk leading to the House. Everything will be kept neat and clean, and every needed attention paid to drainage and sanitary arrangements.

GIVE US A CALL AND SEE.

H. H. CLARK,   -   Prop'r of Island House.

Bear I.

Long Pt.

Deadman's
Pt.

er's
ad

3

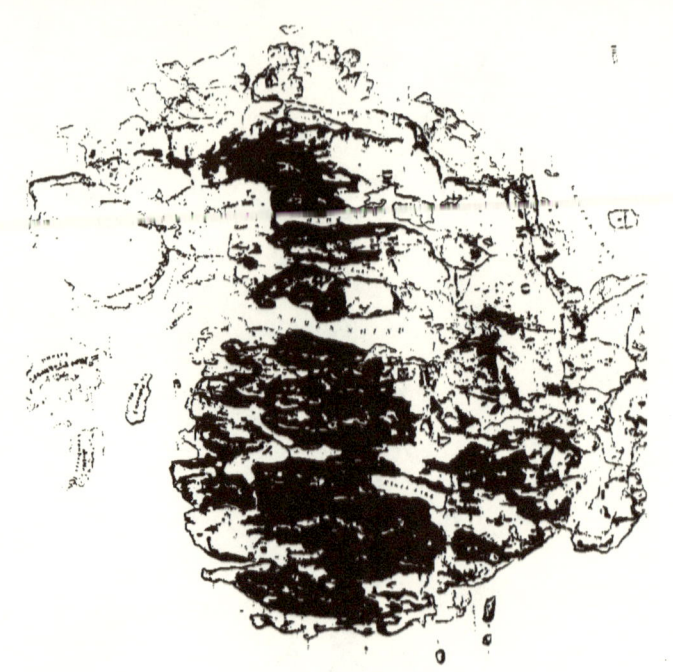